ALL THAT GLITTERS

AN APPLE HILL NOVELLA

JENNIFER SIENES

ISBN: 978-1-951839-12-3

Celebrate Lit Publishing

304 S. Jones Blvd #754

Las Vegas, NV, 89107

http://www.celebratelitpublishing.com/

Chapter 1

Julia

Some dreams are slow to die, and it was often in the wee hours of the morning I would lie awake and ponder how everything went so wrong in my marriage. Did the fifteen extra pounds I carried on my hips, my limp hair, and the attention I gave our eight-year-old play into Stephen's infidelity and lies? I might have been able to do something about the hair and hips but caring for Max was not negotiable.

Understanding how our marriage failed wouldn't change things for Stephen and myself, but it was Max who would ultimately pay the price of an absentee father. I could maybe do something about that, which was why I was quick to accept Stephen's invitation to join him at Apple Hill on that early November day. We hadn't been on a family outing since before the divorce.

We met at Able's Apple Acres where the only things more prevalent than apples were Christmas trees. Fat, skinny, squat and tall ones. The rich fragrance of pine and hay lingered in the cool air. Stephen and I sat on a bench, while I scanned the hay maze for curly blond hair and a red sweatshirt. There were so many people, it would be easy to lose a small boy in the mix.

"We should be hanging out with Max," I said. "He was excited about today's adventure."

"I need to talk to you about something first, Jules," Stephen said.

Dread hijacked my heart rate. The last time he started a conversation like that was when he asked for a divorce, not that he had needed my permission. I took a cleansing breath. "Before you lay something heavy on me, let's get our eyes on Max."

He shifted on the bench, hand clenched on his knee. "I'm sure he's fine."

His impatience nicked at my insecurity, but not enough to be casual with Max's safety. It only took a split second for things to go south. Chatter, laughter, and the delighted squeals of children filled my ears as I continued to search the crowd. I spotted a red shirt and stood to get a clearer view. It was him.

"I was trying to tell you—"

"There he is." I waved, and he waved back as I plopped back onto the bench. "Sorry, Stephen. I know you think I'm a helicopter mom, but if anything happened to him, I'd never forgive myself."

He crossed his arms. "It's fine."

"I'm all yours." Which wasn't really true. I split my attention between him and Max, who was now squatting on the lawn with another little boy while they stared at something on the ground. Who knew what woodland creature they'd found? I'd be sure to check his pockets later.

"Focus, Jules." Stephen's reprimand, although well deserved, made me feel like a child being scolded by her father. "This won't take long, and then you can spend the rest of the day hovering over Max."

"Sorry."

His gaze met mine then slipped away. Was he nervous? In

the fraction of a minute it took him to continue, I'd run the possibilities through my mind. Was he sick? Had he lost his job? Maybe he was getting remarried, which would add a whole new level of complication to the mix.

"I can't seem to get ahead here. The cost of living is ridiculous." He flicked his hand at me. "You know how it is."

"Sure." Financial problems. It's not the first time he'd struggled with making ends meet. Maybe I should have reminded him that he lived beyond his means. On second thought, his choices were none of my business.

"Here's the deal, Jules." He cleared his throat. "I'm moving." Head down, he picked at a spot on his jeans like a kid awaiting a reprimand.

"Okay." So, he was moving. Unless it affected his child support payments, I didn't see why he acted as if I'd object.

"To Arizona."

That was unexpected. Heat, desert, and what? "Why Arizona?"

"There's a job opening with the power company—SRP."

His time with Max was sporadic at best. How would we manage visits back and forth? My guess was Stephen wouldn't put out much effort. First, he abandoned me. Now, he was abandoning his son. Then again, wouldn't it make things easier? Stephen wouldn't look so bad from a thousand miles away.

The moment the thought occurred, shame heated my cheeks. This couldn't be about me. Max was the priority.

"Mesa, to be exact."

It sounded like he had already made up his mind. "Look, Stephen. I know it's expensive here, but you have a good job with PG&E. What will happen to your relationship with Max if you move away?"

I glanced to where I last saw Max and his bug-catching partner, but he wasn't there. I jumped up to search for him. "Do you see him?"

Muttering under his breath, he stood beside me. "At the face-painting booth." He pointed about a hundred yards to the right.

My heart rate settled, and I hooked my purse over my shoulder.

"Where're you going?" He latched onto my upper arm.

I stepped out of his grasp, uneasiness settling in the pit of my stomach. Stephen could be intense, but I sensed this was something else. It would be better to discuss it without distractions. "There are too many people here, and I can't give you my full attention. Let me get Max, and we can find somewhere quiet to talk."

Before he could respond, my phone rang, and I dug through my purse for it. A glance at the caller ID snatched my breath. Katie. She'd only call for an emergency. "What's going on? Is everything okay?"

"It's Tess. She's in labor, and I can't find Jake. Dad and Fiona are down in Sacramento baby shopping, so I'm all alone with her. Can you meet us at the hospital?"

"On my way." I disconnected and reached back into my purse for my keys. "I have to go, Stephen. That was Katie. Tess is in labor." I turned to get my bearings. Which way was the parking lot?

"So? Isn't she old enough to handle it?"

"She's only eighteen. And she's scared."

"Wait a minute." He stepped in front of me. "What about Max?"

"I'll pick him up at your place later. We can talk everything over then." After I had time to process the news.

He shook his head. "I can't take him."

I stared at my boots and drew in a deep breath. Conversations with Stephen were like maneuvering through a minefield. One wrong move and the whole thing would blow up in my face. "Stephen, this is your weekend with Max. He has all his stuff packed and waiting in the car."

"I know, Jules. Sorry. I'll just tell him goodbye and we'll talk more tomorrow."

Marty

It was impossible to line up a putt with a stressed-out father-to-be pacing the green. The truth was, I wished I were in his shoes. What I wouldn't give to be married to a woman rather than to my work, and to be expecting my first child. Of course, just any woman wouldn't do, and the one I wanted gave off the let's-just-be-friends vibe.

"I can't believe you left your phone in the car." There was no doubt Jake thought I was an idiot, but I gave him a pass. If Tess hadn't begged me to get him out of the house for a few hours, I wouldn't have turned traitor on him.

"And I can't believe you left yours back at the house." Not my best comeback.

"I didn't *leave* it. Tess took it from me."

I swung my putter and watched the ball circle the hole before dropping in. The satisfying *plunk* put a smile on my face. "Okay, Tiger, we'll call it a day." There is only so much a man will do for his best friend's wife.

He strode across the green and speared his putter into the golf bag strapped to the back of the cart.

I checked my watch. The longest eight holes I'd ever played. "We would've been done an hour ago if you didn't slice and fade all over the course. What kind of a doctor are you, anyway?"

He scowled. "What're you talking about?"

I snatched my ball from the hole, pocketed it, and meandered to the golf cart. "Any doctor worth his salt should be a good golfer."

"That's like saying all accountants are stick-in-the-mud bores."

He had me there.

"Can we get back to the house now?"

"Just following the boss's orders. If you weren't standing over your poor wife like she couldn't manage to cross the room on her own, she wouldn't have kicked you out of the house without your phone."

Jake muttered something I couldn't quite catch as he climbed into the cart.

"What's that?"

"I said this is ridiculous. She could have the baby any day now, and she kicks me out. The one person who could actually be of use if she goes into labor early."

Before my rear hit the seat beside him, we were moving.

"I'll remind you of this someday when you have a kid of your own." Jake glowered at me, pushing the cart to maximum speed.

"You want to slow this thing down? I'd like to make it there in one piece." But I was talking to a wall.

We got to the parking lot in record time, and while I loaded the golf bags into the back of my Jeep, Jake retrieved my phone.

"Here." He shoved it at me.

I woke the phone. Three missed calls, but none from Tess. "Isn't this Katie's number?" I turned the screen his way.

His eyes widened. "I *knew* this was going to happen."

I handed him the phone. "Call her back and get into the Jeep."

"I'm driving."

I hooked Jake's arm before he could plant himself in the driver's seat. "Not on my watch, pal. I'd like to live long enough to have those hypothetical kids you were talking about."

Jake glared at me but rounded the front of the vehicle to

the passenger side. Before he got his seatbelt buckled, he was on the phone with Katie.

"How's she doing?" He listened for a moment. "Yeah. Uh huh. We're on our way. No, sorry. Marty left his phone in the car. Tell her I love her."

Jake grumbled the entire fifteen minutes it took to get to the hospital. I pulled up to the front entrance, and the Jeep was barely in park before he bolted. "Meet you inside," I yelled, but I was the last thing he was thinking about.

I found a parking space and took a more leisurely pace through the hospital, following directions on the wall for the Birth Center. Katie sat in the waiting room with Max. Julia must be in with Tess. There wasn't anyone else around.

When Katie spotted me, she jumped up. "What took you so long?" She combed her fingers through her long red hair, green eyes clouded with worry. "She wasn't supposed to have the baby for a couple of weeks. I couldn't get ahold of Dad, and you didn't answer your phone."

I slung a casual arm around her shoulder. "Relax, Kitkat. Having babies is as natural as breathing."

"Do tell." Julia strode into the room. "When you have the ability to push an eight-pound bowling ball with limbs from your body, then we'll be all ears."

Katie latched onto her. "How is she?"

Julia chuckled. "Relax. Having babies is as natural as breathing."

"Hey." I faced off with her, ready to launch into my spiel. "You just—"

"Bup!" She pointed at me. "Not a word."

I shook my head and looked at Max. "Are you hungry?"

"Starving."

"Let's go see what we can find to eat. It's obvious we're not appreciated here."

"Hey, Marty?" Julia smiled at me. "Can I talk to you a minute?"

She had a favor to ask, and as long as it wasn't helping out in the birthing room, I was game.

"Sure." We stepped into the hallway, and I leaned against the wall. As short as she was, she had to look up to bat those brown eyes at me—rich and dark, like the double-chocolate ice cream Gramps and I used to share. "What's up?"

"What are the chances you'd take Max back up to Apple Hill? We never got to Delphino Farms or looked at Christmas trees or even got anything to eat. Stephen was supposed to keep him this weekend, but…" She waved her hand in the air as if to erase the next thought.

"No problem."

She touched my forearm. "You're a lifesaver, Marty. I'm sure I'll still be here, so you can drop him off after."

The heat radiating from her hand hijacked my brain for a moment. Not the first time. Wouldn't be the last. We'd been playing this friend game for a couple of years, and I wanted more. I just had to find a way to convince her.

"You're sure you don't mind?"

I rallied long enough to retrieve my mental faculties. "I'd much rather hang out with Max than sit in a waiting room."

"Just remember, he can't eat—"

"Peanuts. I know. I'll be sure he's allergy-free before I return him to you."

She gave me a megawatt smile. "Could you pick up a couple crates of apples, too?"

The woman had no shame.

Chapter 2

Julia

The precious bundle in my arms flooded me with the desire to have another of my own but being auntie to my best friend's baby would have to suffice. I whisper-touched the tuft of red hair, and looked at Tess, propped up in the hospital bed. Her cheeks were pink, hair pulled into a haphazard ponytail.

"He's beautiful, Tess." My smile was so big, my cheeks hurt. I touched my lips to his wrinkled forehead. "Sean Patrick Holland, you've got the best mama and daddy in the whole world."

"He's something, isn't he?"

"He is that."

"I've never seen Jake so rattled." Tess laughed. "I hope he's more composed in the emergency room than he was with me."

A memory flitted across my mind. "Do you remember the day at the restaurant when Katie choked on something?"

"A cherry tomato." Tess shifted her position, a grimace marring her face. "She was throwing them in the air and catching them in her mouth. I think that was the scariest day of my life."

"Mine, too. But Jake wasn't ruffled in the least. He did that procedure—"

"A cricothyrotomy."

"Whatever." I shook my head. "He was amazing. You're both amazing." Tears burned my eyes, and I blinked them away.

"Hey, what's with the tears?"

"They're happy tears. Mostly." Aside from that part of me grieving over a life I'd never have.

"Mostly?"

Sean squirmed, and I readjusted him in my arms. "Forget I said that. It must be the close proximity to newborns and the upcoming holidays."

"Come on, Jules." She tilted her head. "When have we ever kept things from each other?"

I raised my eyebrows at her. Words weren't necessary.

She waved her hand as if to dismiss my thoughts. "Aside from that."

I frowned. "Don't make light of it, Tess." For ten years she kept her rape from me and stayed mired in the shame and fear, unable to move forward until her dad took drastic measures.

"You're deflecting."

"Don't pull your psychobabble on me." I looked down at the baby. "I take it back, Sean. Your mother's going to drive you nuts before you hit puberty."

"Come on, Jules. Out with it. What's going on?"

I placed Sean in the bassinet at the end of Tess's hospital bed then crossed to the window that overlooked the parking lot. The sun-bathed the sky in hues of pink and orange. "I always had this idea of what my life would be like, you know what I mean?" I faced her again.

She hooked a strand of wayward hair behind her ear and nodded. "You're preaching to the choir, sister."

"I'm sorry, Tess. I wasn't thinking."

"Stop." She patted the bed beside her. "Sit down and talk to me."

I eased onto the bed, careful not to bump her. "Stephen's moving to Arizona."

A wrinkle formed between her brows. "Arizona? Why?"

"Who knows? He says it's because he can't afford to live here anymore, but I'm sure there's more to it. There always is with him."

"Okay." She touched my hand. "It's not like you're still in love with him."

I made a rude noise in my throat. "Absolutely not. That boat sailed long ago. What concerns me is Max. He needs his dad, even if it's an occasional thing. Do you know the statistics about boys raised without their fathers?"

"No."

"Neither do I, but I'm sure it's not good. Stephen hardly knew his father, and I'm sure that plays a huge role in the struggles he has today."

"Max needs a father figure, and Stephen's never been much of one to him. Is that such a great loss?"

"Maybe not, but Stephen is the only one he has," I said. "Even if he's a disappointment. As it is, Max is getting used to his dad not showing up for visits. It's like he almost expects it. He didn't even balk when he found out he had to come to the hospital with me instead of staying up the hill with his dad."

"What about Marty?"

I squinted at Tess. Was she serious? "What about him?"

"He's great with Max."

"True, but it's not like anyone can ever take Stephen's place in Max's heart, even if Max isn't aware of it now. Your mom and dad were so good to me, but I still yearned for my own parents to be proud of me. Besides, Marty is just a friend."

"Just a friend, huh? Give me a break, Jules. You've had a thing for him since he came into the picture."

I couldn't deny it. His laid back, surfer-boy looks combined with an accountant's brain was an attractive package. And he made me laugh. "If you remember correctly, Marty had a thing for you."

She shook her head. "That was nothing."

"Even so, he has no interest in me. And even if he did, I'm not about to make the same mistake twice."

"Meaning what?"

"The hardest thing I've ever gone through was Stephen's infidelity."

"I know that." She touched my hand. "Does that mean you're never going to remarry? You'd spend your life alone rather than take a chance on loving again?"

"If I knew it meant not suffering the humiliation of another divorce? Absolutely."

"Oh, Jules. Don't use Stephen's failure as a husband to color every other relationship you might have. That's not fair to you or to whomever you could have a future with. You were the one who pushed me to give Jake a chance and look at us now."

"That's not the same."

"Sure it is."

It would do no good to point out the differences in our physicality. Tess walked down the street, even nine months pregnant, and turned men's heads. I did not. "You two are a good match," I said.

She frowned. "You've always sold yourself short, Jules. I wish you could see yourself the way I see you. The way God sees you."

I smiled and shook a finger at her to lighten the mood. "Don't even think about quoting Psalm 139:14 to me again."

"One of these days, you'll believe it."

Marty

It was a calmer Jake who sat in the passenger seat as we drove to Bella Cucina's. Calmer, but a little loopy. Was that what fatherhood did to a guy? I'd taken pity on Tess and strong-armed Jake into accompanying me to the restaurant. The old-fashioned streetlamps along Main Street gave the downtown area a sense of the days of yore. In another couple weeks, the street would be decked with greenery, velvet bows and a twenty-foot Christmas tree next to the bell tower. A real Norman Rockwell experience.

"I don't want to be gone long," Jake reminded me for the tenth time in as many minutes.

"How does it feel to be a father?"

"Terrifying."

That wasn't the answer I'd expected. "What're you afraid of?"

"Everything from a hangnail to SIDS."

There wasn't a man I knew who had it together as well as Jake. "Whatever comes along, you can handle it. Besides, you have your family, lots of friends and your faith."

"You sound like Tess."

"She's right. I've no doubt you'll be a great dad." When he didn't respond, I threw him a bone. "We'll leave the apples in the kitchen, pick up some food for you two, and head back. Promise."

"Tell me again why you have two crates of apples? I didn't listen."

I wasn't about to touch that remark. "Julia asked me to pick them up when I took Max to Apple Hill. She said something about Maris using them in some fancy desserts for this week's specials."

"And the live Christmas tree on the back seat?"

"Max picked it out. I thought Julia would like it for her house. I'll drop it off at her place tomorrow."

He chuckled. "Instead of saying it with flowers, you're saying it with a Christmas tree. Do everyone a favor and tell her how you feel."

"We're just friends."

He barked out a laugh. "Did you forget who you're talking to? How many times did I use that line on you when you told me to come clean about Tess?"

"Okay, so I have feelings for her, but the timing isn't right."

Jake snorted. "It never is."

I turned into the alley behind Bella Cucina's and parked. Back doors to the businesses on this block of Main Street lined up like teeth on a jack-o'-lantern, each with a light fixture above. There was enough wattage to make out dumpsters, but not enough to chase away the shadows. "Do you have your key?"

"Oh, no. Sorry. I guess we'll have to go to the house to get it." Loopy and absentminded. Who could blame him?

"No problem. I have Julia's."

Even in the dim interior, I caught his glare. "Then why am I here?"

"You have the alarm code, and I thought you could use the distraction. First Tess's family and now Julia. There's only so much baby googly-eyes a man can take. By the time we get back, everyone will be gone, and you can cozy up to your wife and son in peace. I'm doing you a favor."

He sighed. "It may not seem like it, but I appreciate it. I clock more hours at the hospital than I do at home." He climbed out of the Jeep.

I rounded the back and popped the latch.

Jake reached in for a crate of apples. "What's wrong with the timing?"

"Huh?" I hauled out the second one and led the way to the door.

"With Julia," Jake said to my back. "Is it Max?"

"Of course not. He's a great kid. It's Stephen." After placing the crate on the ground, I reached in my pocket for the keys. "I don't need the ghost of their marriage haunting us. I just need to be sure he's in the past before I put myself out there."

Jake pushed the door open. "He'll never be in the past. He's Max's dad."

"You go first." I followed Jake and kicked the door closed behind us. "I don't mean in Max's past. I mean Julia's. I may only have one shot with her, and I don't want to blow it."

With a flick of a switch, the kitchen lit up. Stainless steel was the color of choice—industrial-size refrigerator, cooktops, ovens, and massive oven vents. Pans, hung from a rack in the middle of the room, lessened the severity.

I put my crate of apples next to Jake's on the island counter. "Hard to believe you were running this joint when we met."

"Yep. Being an E.R. doc is child's play in comparison. But I wouldn't trade it for the world."

"Well, yeah, you got Tess out of the deal."

He folded his arms. "I know for a fact that Julia's not hung up on her ex, if that's what's got you hesitating."

"Maybe not, but she's still letting their relationship color her thinking. Until she trusts me, she's not going to let me in. Slow and steady wins the race, my friend."

Chapter 3

Julia

Gray clouds darkened the morning sky and fed my premonition of doom after a sleepless night of wrestling with an invisible foe—much like Jacob did the Angel of the Lord. Only my foe wasn't divine, all-powerful, or righteous. Mine was an ex-husband whose only consistency was being inconsistent.

By 3:00 a.m., I gave up the ghost, so to speak, and climbed out of bed. By six, I had a week's worth of meals made and ready to take to Tess, along with two loaves of bread and a batch of muffins. By eight, a pot of soup was cooling on the stovetop, and I was showered, dressed and ready for battle.

"Aren't we going to church?" Max rubbed sleep from his eyes as I hustled him into the kitchen.

"Not this morning, sweetie. We're going to take some food to Aunt Tess's and then stop by your dad's."

"Okay."

I set him at the table with fruit, yogurt, and a muffin then returned to his bedroom to gather his clothes while I tapped Stephen's number on my phone for the third time.

"The voicemail is full. Please try again later."

I clenched my teeth at the robotic tone. Why wasn't Stephen picking up? And when had he ever gotten enough calls to fill his voicemail? I slipped the phone into my back pocket and straightened Max's bedroom.

The last thing I wanted was to cause more strife between Stephen and me and showing up unannounced was a sure-fire way to set him off. I was tired of acting like the insecure wallflower I'd been when we were married, but the idea of a confrontation with him set my stomach roiling.

"I'm done." Max stood in the doorway, no longer sleepy-eyed.

"Great. Brush your teeth, get dressed, and we'll be on our way."

While Max got ready, I found a box for the food and put it in the back seat of my car. I didn't expect Tess would be home from the hospital until later in the day, so I'd be able to slip in and out.

When we arrived at Tess's, Max helped carry the food through the back door, and I rearranged the refrigerator to fit it all. Although I had no doubt Tess's dad, Sean, would provide enough food until baby Sean graduated high school, I didn't know how else to help.

"Okay kiddo, next stop."

We arrived at Stephen's before I was prepared for the face-off. All night long, I'd practiced logical arguments in my mind, but as I parked in a guest spot, I couldn't think of a single one. If Stephen was determined to move, there was nothing I could do about it.

"Are we gonna see Dad?" Max looked up from the book in his lap—*5000 Awesome Facts.*

"Yes." If he was there. "Grab your jacket."

The building was swanky by Placerville standards, but not nearly as expensive as the Eldorado Hills condo we'd lived in before our divorce. Still, Stephen was all about image, especially when it far exceeded reality.

With a hand pressed to my stomach, I gave Max a smile and rapped on Stephen's door. Nothing. It was after 9:30, but it was possible he was still asleep. Waking him wouldn't improve his mood any, but at this point, what did it matter? I could be a timid little field mouse begging for crumbs or a protective mama bear fighting for the rights of her son. I fisted my hand and pounded loud enough to wake the neighbors. Still nothing.

"Isn't he home?" Max knocked. "Hey, Dad!"

"Maybe he's still sleeping, sweetie." I rummaged in my purse for my phone and keys. Another attempt to reach him got me the same voicemail message. I'd never used the key to Stephen's apartment, and I hesitated to do so now. I wouldn't like it if he invaded my privacy, and yet, we'd swapped keys for a reason. I pushed aside my doubts and unlocked the door.

Before I could poke my head in, Max pushed through the door. I started to call out, but the words were snatched before they left my mouth. No furniture. No pictures on the wall. No throw rugs. Nothing.

"Where's his stuff?" Max ran down the hall out of sight.

"What is going on?" Even whispered, the question bounced against the stark emptiness. It was like I'd landed in the middle of a Twilight Zone episode. My footsteps echoed on the hardwood floor as I strode across the living room and into the cherrywood and granite kitchen. Aside from a crumb or two, the cabinets were bare.

It was as if Stephen hadn't been there at all.

Marty

The three-foot Christmas tree in its glossy red pot mocked me from the passenger seat of my Jeep. Amazing. It sounded uncannily like Jake. I must've been suffering from some form of mental illness, which should've warned me this wasn't my brightest idea. My only defense was that I'd been out of practice with the fairer sex, and flowers would've been too obvious.

The last thing I wanted was to make Julia uncomfortable.

Her house was a white farmhouse style with red shutters. It was a small place, but if memory served, still plenty of space for my driving companion. I disentangled the seatbelt from the pot and climbed out of the Jeep. Hugging the tree to my chest, I carried it to the front door. Worst case, Julia could always leave it on the wide porch.

There was no scamper of little Max feet in response to the doorbell. I set the tree down and turned to leave when Julia's car pulled into the driveway.

Max exploded from the passenger seat. "Hey, Marty. I forgot you were coming today." He plowed up the front steps.

"Munchkin Max. You just getting home from church?"

"Nuh-uh." He stepped up to the tree and fingered the needles. "We took some food to Aunt Tess's and then went to my dad's. You brought my tree."

Julia stopped at the bottom of the stairs and pointed. "What's that?" There was something in her voice or body language that was off. Did she and Stephen have an argument?

I stuck my nose in the air and used my best snotty-professor voice. "This, my dear, is a *picea pungens*."

Max wrinkled his nose. "Huh?"

I broke character and grinned. "That's the scientific name for a blue spruce."

Shaking her head, Julia climbed the steps. "Do I even want to know how you came by this source of information?"

"Probably not. However, I thought you might like it. It's really the perfect Christmas tree—the gift that keeps on giving." Could I sound any lamer?

"Well." Her eyes, suspiciously moist, didn't quite meet

mine. "That's sweet of you." Reaching around me, she unlocked the door. "Would you like to come in?"

"I don't know. Would you like me to?" It might be better to cut and run while I still could.

Max slid between us to get inside. "I'm starving."

"Of course you are." A smile flirted at the edge of Julia's mouth despite the tears that dampened her lashes.

In the two years or so Julia and I had been friends, I'd seen her many moods in various forms—anger, protectiveness, comical, warm, and cold. I'd even seen her laugh so hard, she had to rush to the bathroom. But I'd never seen her cry. "Are you okay?" Not my brightest depth-probing question, but better than ignoring the situation, which was what I was tempted to do.

She held the door open for me. "Enter, if you dare."

I stepped into the family room, and she closed the door behind me. "What's going on, Jules?"

"Let me go check on Max first. Can I get you anything to drink? Or, I have homemade soup. I can nuke it if you'd like."

"Let's talk first."

She followed Max into the kitchen while I settled on the couch. The room was tidy, aside from clothes spilling out of a laundry basket in the corner. The furniture was old but seemed to be in good condition. I didn't imagine Julia had money for many extras.

Julia appeared and sat in a rocker across from me. "He's going to eat me out of house and home." She swiped at a dark strand of hair with trembling fingers and cleared her throat. "I swear he had a decent breakfast. At this rate, he'll need a whole new wardrobe before Christmas."

"You want to tell me what's got you so upset?"

Her gaze flickered toward the kitchen then back at me. "This was supposed to be Stephen's weekend with Max, not that it makes much difference. Max is lucky if he gets a weekend a month with his dad."

I rested my elbows on my knees. "Is that why you're upset?"

She gave a quick jerk of her head. "Yesterday, he told me he's moving to Arizona."

Ahh. Now it was making sense. Could Jake have been misinformed? A heaviness sat in my gut at the thought.

"We didn't get a chance to discuss it because Tess went into labor. So, I went by this morning to talk to him, but he wasn't there."

"Well, maybe he was out."

"No." A quick glance at the kitchen and she lowered her voice. "The apartment is completely empty. There's not enough left to keep a mouse alive for a day. It's as if he was never there."

Okay, that was a little weird. "When did he say he was moving?"

"He didn't, but I got the impression he'd just made the decision. There's no way he emptied out the apartment between the time we met yesterday and when I showed up this morning."

"What are you saying?" Good riddance to bad rubbish as far as I was concerned. But maybe that was my self-centered heart talking.

"I don't know. It doesn't make any sense. Something just doesn't add up."

Chapter 4

Julia

Somehow, one night of sleeplessness had always given me the ability to be hyper-focused. There must've been a scientific reason, but I'd yet to find it. Two nights with no sleep, however, turned me into a bona-fide zombie, which was not how I wanted to face a day of bookkeeping at the restaurant. All night, the image of Stephen's empty apartment haunted me. Should I call his mother? Maybe I should report it to the police. Was he on the run from something or suffering from some form of mental illness?

And even in the light of day, as I stared at QuickBooks on my work computer, questions plagued me.

A quick rap on the door and Maris stuck her pink-bandana-covered head in. "Hey, Jules. Thanks for the apples. How much do I owe you?"

Apples? I ran her comment through my befuddled, caffeine-spiked brain. Marty. Apple Hill. How could I have forgotten? "I'll find out. Marty picked them up for me."

She wriggled her eyebrows and stepped inside, her linebacker-sized body filling the small space. "Is there something you're not telling me?"

I rubbed my burning eyes with a thumb and forefinger and stifled a groan. She was as bad as Tess. "We're just friends."

"Sure you are."

"Why doesn't anyone believe me?"

Crossing her arms, she leaned against the wall. "Maybe because Tess and I are more intuitive than you."

"I didn't say anything about Tess."

"You didn't have to." She grinned. "But I'll take mercy on you and let it go. Back to the apples. Do you have some ideas about dessert specials leading up to Thanksgiving?"

"I do, but I need to get some bills paid and the accounts reconciled before I put on my sous-chef hat."

She narrowed her eyes at me. "It looks to me like you could use a strong cup of coffee."

I snagged the oversized mug sitting on my desk and held it up. "This is my third. Once it kicks in, I'll be Wonder Woman again. Until then, my bleary-eyed alter ego will have to suffice."

"Long night?"

"You could say that. Give me an hour or so, and I'll meet you in the kitchen."

She glanced at her watch. "Make it two. The lunch crowd's going to be here soon."

"Do you need help?" *Please say no.*

"Katie doesn't have classes today, so she's here." She reached across my desk and nabbed the mug. "I'll get you a refresher."

An hour later, I was closing out QuickBooks when Katie popped in. For the brief moment it took my eyes to focus, she looked like Tess's twin rather than her much younger sister.

"Hey, Katie. Have you talked to Tess today?"

"Yeah, and she's doing good. Are you going by after work?"

"That's the plan. I'm afraid if I call, I'll wake her or the baby."

She laughed. "Like Jake will let that happen. He's shooting for the overprotective dad of the year award. He needs to go back to work. Anyway, there's some guy out front who wants to talk to you."

Stephen. Relief eased the tension in my shoulders. "Send him back, will you?"

"Sure."

I stood to stretch then gathered the receipts and bills into a pile. Now that Stephen was here, all the doom and gloom scenarios I'd created in my mind seemed ridiculous. Talk about an overactive imagination. Thankfully, I hadn't shared them with anyone, so my embarrassment could die with me. Movement at the door drew my attention.

"Steph—" My voice was cut off by the sight of a stranger looming in the doorway. He was taller than Maris, which put him far above me, and although he was smiling, a chill skittered up my spine. "Uh, sorry. I was expecting someone else."

"Your husband?"

"Ex-husband," I said as I crossed my arms and took a step back. The heel of my foot struck the bookshelf behind me. Was this what a trapped animal felt like? Here I was, overreacting again. Maris was within shouting distance, and there must've been more than twenty patrons in the dining room. I blamed lack of sleep. "Who are you?"

"Glen. I'm a friend of Stephen's." He held out a hand. "You must be Julia."

I hesitated a beat or two before accepting his handshake. Red flags waved like a color guard presentation, but what else could I do? "Yes, I am. Why are you here?" The question was ripe with suspicion. Being a friend of Stephen's didn't earn Glen any brownie points as far as I was concerned.

Like a used car salesman hoping to make a score, his smile didn't waver. "I owe him some money but can't seem to get ahold of him."

Join the club. "I'd be happy to help."

The ever-present smile finally reached his eyes. "Great."

"You can leave the money with me, and I'll be sure he gets it."

So much for the warmth in his eyes. "I really need to talk to him about it first. Maybe come up with a payment plan."

If he owed Stephen money then I was tall, thin and rich. More than likely, it was the other way around. "If you're a friend of his, you must have his phone number."

"Sure. But I can't seem to reach him."

"Well, Glen, I'm not sure how I can help."

"How about an address?"

"That, I can do." I rattled off the street and number of Stephen's abandoned apartment and watched Glen's smile melt away. Apparently, he was already privy to that information and the fact that no one was there anymore.

A muscle tightened in his jaw, and his fingers twitched at his side like a gunfighter preparing to draw. "I was hoping for his forwarding address."

"I'm afraid I don't have it." Even if I did, I wouldn't share it with him. Why I felt a need to protect Stephen was beyond me. Maybe it was because this guy made my skin prickle.

Marty

The more I thought about Stephen's disappearing act, the more bizarre it seemed. He told Julia he'd planned to move away, but then to disappear overnight? Had he planned it out weeks ago, and the last step was telling her? Or was he in trouble? Knowing Julia the way I did, and how she erred on the side of grace—I would've been hard pressed to muster sympathy for him.

But still, he was Max's father, which made him important to Julia, so unless he'd made a miraculous reappearance, she was probably freaking out. That was all the excuse I needed to detour to Bella Cucina on my way to Sacramento.

I parked next to her car in the alley and slipped in the back door. The Eagles' "The Long Run" competed with clatter in the kitchen, and a couple of waitresses dressed in traditional black pants and white shirts, arms laden with trays of mouth-watering food, zipped down the hallway.

"Are you looking for Julia?" Jeanine or Jeri or some other J-name stopped at the kitchen entrance, balancing a load bigger than her.

"Do you need help with that?" I stepped closer, arms out as if to take it from her. What I'd do with it then, I had no idea.

"I'm good." She pointed her chin down the hall. "Julia's in her office." She lowered her voice. "There's some guy in with her, so we've been keeping an eye out."

I grimaced. Stephen, no doubt. Good to know they had her back. "Thanks." It was hard to hear clearly with classic rock booming from the kitchen, but I caught the rumble of a deep voice as I approached Julia's office. I'd never met Stephen, but something in my gut told me it wasn't him towering over her desk.

I stopped at the door since moving inside would put me nose to shoulder with the guy. "Hey, Jules."

Julia peeked around his imposing form as he turned to me. Her face lit up like it was Christmas morning, and she blew out a shaky breath. "Come on in, Marty. Glen was just leaving."

"Glen, is it?" I gave him a grin and a comradely slap on the shoulder. "What brings you here?"

"He's looking for Stephen." Julia pushed out her chin.

"Well, Glen,"—I gave him a pointed look—"good luck with that." I stepped aside so he could exit and watched until he disappeared into the dining room. Bravado aside, I wouldn't want to meet him in a dark alley.

"I'm so glad you showed up." Julia dropped into the desk chair, her usual olive complexion now a pasty white. "Not that I was in any danger."

"You weren't." I jerked a thumb over my shoulder. "The staff had your back. What's his deal, anyway?" I rested a hip on the edge of the desk.

She ran a trembling hand over her face. "I don't know. He says he's a friend of Stephen's, but…" She shrugged. "He's lying. I just don't know why."

"Well, he's gone now." But for how long? "Are you okay? You don't look so good."

She gave me a crooked smile. "Just what a girl wants to hear. Thanks."

"You know what I mean. You're always beautiful, even with dark circles under your eyes. But you look like a slight breeze could take you down." I blurted the compliment without thinking.

"Oh, uh…" She dropped her gaze and shuffled the pile on her desk. "I didn't sleep well last night. Or the night before."

I'd made her uncomfortable, but I had to take a chance sometime, even if it was a minuscule one. "Not sleeping, huh? I suppose it's natural to be worried about him." Was I trying to convince her or myself?

"Him? You mean Stephen?"

"I'm not talking about your new friend, Glen."

She frowned. "I'm not quite that altruistic. I mean, he's Max's dad, and of course I don't want anything to happen to him, but if I'm going to be completely honest with you—"

"Always."

She laid her hands flat on the desk. "I'm equally angry

with him, because as sure as we're sitting here, he's gotten himself involved in something he shouldn't have."

"I don't get it." I yanked a chair from the corner, set it in front of her desk, and sat. "Why him?"

"What do you mean?"

How could I ask without making it awkward for both of us? "We know each other pretty well, don't you think?"

She sat at her desk. "I think so."

"You're a devoted mom, loyal friend, great cook, dependable employee, and hardworking. Did I miss anything?"

"I don't know. Are you planning on having me canonized?" She grimaced, but her cheeks were pink, and her eyes didn't quite meet mine.

"Sorry if I embarrassed you. The point I'm awkwardly leading up to is that I don't get what attracted you to Stephen in the first place. I mean, unless there's something I'm missing."

She cocked her head and squinted. "Are you the same person you were ten years ago?"

"Ten years ago?" Where was I ten years ago? It was before Gillian or my time with Gramps. Even I wouldn't have recognized myself back then. "Thankfully, no."

"Neither was I. But if I had it to do all over again, I wouldn't change a thing, because I wouldn't have Max."

"Point taken."

"But you can bet I won't make the same mistake twice."

Was that supposed to be some kind of warning?

Chapter 5

Julia

I was frozen in the entryway to Tess's living room, with an arm slung over Max's shoulders. The glow from a table lamp in the corner and strategically placed candles chased away the late afternoon gloom. If that wasn't strange enough, vibrant pillows sat like dutiful soldiers along the back of her white sofa. Either Tess had been nesting or Jake had gone off the deep end.

"What's wrong?" Tess stopped in the middle of the room, her bare toes curling into the plush, emerald-toned area rug.

"Just admiring how your maternal nature's exploded all over the place."

"Very funny."

"I've never in my life seen you buy a throw pillow."

"Never say never. Are you going to come in or did you just stop by to insult me?"

"It wasn't an insult. More like a backhanded compliment. Mind if I get Max a snack?"

"You know your way around my kitchen better than I do, Jules. Please help yourself."

I squeezed Max's shoulder. "Come on, kiddo, let's see what we can find you."

Five minutes later, I had Max settled at the kitchen table. "You do your homework while I talk to Aunt Tess." I deposited a plate of sliced apples and cheese in front of him, attempted to ruffle his dodging head, and returned to the family room.

Tess was curled up in the corner of the sofa, hugging a bright yellow pillow. "Sorry for being so lazy, but I figured you didn't need my help."

"Well, I don't know what your problem is. It's not like you just had a baby or anything." I burrowed myself into the opposite corner. It would've been so easy to slide down a little further and take a quick cat nap.

Jake sauntered in from the back of the house in jeans and flannel shirt with a white spit-up rag hanging off one shoulder. He was a magazine cover for a cross between *GQ* and *This Old House*. "Hey, Julia. I didn't realize you were here. Where's Max?" He sat on the arm of the couch and touched Tess's shoulder.

I waved a lazy hand toward the kitchen. "Doing his home-work. We won't stay long," I said around a sudden yawn.

Tess's soft laughter drew my attention. "We can put you down for a nap with Sean. It looks like you could use it."

"I'm afraid once I go down, I'm not getting back up until morning. How's everything going with you guys? For brand new parents, you look pretty comfortable."

Tess dropped her head back onto Jake's thigh and looked up at him. "Teamwork, right babe?"

He gave her a crooked smile and touched the tip of her nose. Could they be more nauseating? "Yep. At least for the next week. Then I'm back at work."

"You don't sound too excited about it."

He shrugged. "I love my job, but it doesn't compare to being a dad, you know?"

Actually, I didn't know, because Stephen never seemed to take to it. "There's nothing that says you can't be a house husband."

Tess leaned forward. "Oh, yes, there is. Unless he wants to live off a teacher's salary. College tuition is only eighteen short years away."

Would I have sounded bitter if I reminded her I had almost half that time—with less than half the income—to pull a rabbit from a hat? "Tell me about it," I said. "I suppose there's always trade school."

Tess grimaced. "We can strategize all we want, but it's not us who's ultimately in charge. God's got a plan for Max. Speaking of... did you get the scoop on Stephen's big move? I still can't believe he'd want to live so far away."

I glanced behind me to be sure Max hadn't wandered in. "No scoop. No Stephen."

Jake furrowed his brow. "What do you mean?"

"I tried calling a half a dozen times yesterday morning, but I couldn't even leave a message. So, I went by his apartment, and it's empty."

"Empty?" Tess sat up. "You mean like he moved, empty?"

"Like he was never even there, empty." A fist sat in my throat making it hard to breathe.

Jake rose and pulled the rag from his shoulder. "He didn't leave a forwarding address or a way to reach him?"

"No. To top it off, his child support payment wasn't deposited to my account over the weekend. He set it up, so it'd be automatically deducted from his paycheck on the fifteenth."

Jake twisted the rag in his hands as if he wanted to strangle someone with it. Stephen would've been my guess, and his protectiveness comforted me somehow.

Tess reached over and took Jake's wrist, guiding him to sit again. "What about his mom? Have you contacted her?"

"Only as a last resort, and I'm not that desperate yet. You

know how strained things have been between Margaret and me since the divorce."

A cry erupted from down the hall, and Jake jumped up. "I'll take care of phase one."

Tess watched him leave, a gentle smile on her face. "He's a keeper." She turned back to me. "Now that he's gone, tell me why you're really here, and make it quick. He'll have Sean's diaper changed in less than five minutes."

After more than twenty years as my best friend, it no longer surprised me when Tess clued in to the nuances of my thoughts. "It's about Marty. I think you might be right about him having feelings for me, and I'm not sure what to do."

Tess's grin rivaled that of the Cheshire Cat. "I knew it. What did he say?"

"Nothing obvious. But it's kind of out of character for him to show up at the restaurant like he did. And he stopped by the house on Sunday to bring me a Christmas tree, of all things."

"Jake told me about the tree. Marty can be spontaneous. Did he say anything out of character?"

Could we sound more middle school if we tried? "Does telling me I'm beautiful count?" Heat stole up my neck. When was the last time a man said I was beautiful?

Tess clapped her hands. "I knew it."

"I'm glad one of us is giddy about it." I stood to pace. "He's been a really good friend, Tess. I don't want to mess that up."

"Just take it slow and see how things play out."

"You make it sound easy."

"And you make things harder than they have to be. One day at a time, sweetie. I know you feel that your instincts are off when it comes to men, but God's got a plan for you, too."

❄

Marty

The drive to Sacramento was uneventful—not nearly as tough as finding a parking space near the Urban Outreach. Downtown was a mixture of the haves and the have-nots. The gold sphere-topped Capitol Building, inspired by the one in D.C., sat on twelve blocks of groomed gardens. It was surrounded by swanky and not so swanky restaurants and bars, Downtown Commons, and the extravagant Golden One Center.

But it was the have-nots that drew my interest. Homeless, hungry and desperate.

Walking the four blocks from my parking space to the outreach center, I came across five men aimlessly wandering the streets—each one chained to their past mistakes or present circumstances—their eyes vacant of hope. *There but for the grace of God go I.* Every time I journeyed to the center, Gramps' voice reminded me it wasn't enough to just be thankful. "Faith without works is dead," he would say.

The ripe smell of unwashed bodies greeted me when I stepped into the building. The two benches that flanked the hallway were filled to capacity with people in various shades of disarray.

I nodded and smiled to each as I passed. "How are you doing? Someone will be with you as soon as possible. Thanks for your patience." I would've wagered most of them had nowhere else to be. The large interior room was a chaos of cheap desks and chairs, rundown office equipment, volunteers, and clients. There wasn't much money to spend on appearances when resources were in such high demand.

Carol, a bird-of-a-woman, approached. "Marty. Good, you're early. We're short-staffed today."

"Let me just find an empty desk and get my laptop up and running."

Placing a hand on my arm, she took a breath. "I'm sorry. I

didn't even say hello." She smiled. "My husband is always telling me I need to learn the art of conversation. So, hello."

I put an arm around her shoulders and gave her a side hug. "Hi. And you're fine. I'm not offended in the least. There are more needs than time." I looked over her frizzy hair and spotted an empty table. "Give me one minute and then send the next person in."

I passed occupied desks, smiling and waving my way to the corner station. It took less than thirty seconds to arrange my computer and forms on the scarred oak table. Either its legs were uneven, or the floor was, and every time I touched it, it tilted and hit the ground with a *thump*. It was annoying, but a reminder that nothing in life was perfect—except for the Creator. And no one knew this more than the multitude of people waiting to be served.

My first meeting was with Amber, who needed financial counseling.

"I found myself a job." She offered a soft smile and brushed a thin strand of blond hair off her face. "It's not much, but if I can figure out a budget, I think it'll work."

"That's great news, Amber."

"If it hadn't been for Marcy over there"—she waved a hand in the direction of another volunteer— "I don't think they'd have looked twice at my application."

"That's what we're here for. Let's start with your income." I took up a pen and slid a yellow legal pad in front of me. "What's your monthly salary?"

She shrugged. "It varies. It's waitressing, so some days I make more than others."

"Then why don't we start with the base pay?"

I jotted down the numbers before plugging them into a form on the computer. When I first volunteered, I was amazed that anyone could live off so little. But a couple of years stepping into hard cases had desensitized me some.

"I was getting child support, but then my ex quit his job,

so he won't have to pay no more." Her eyes were shiny with unshed tears—another thing I'd gotten used to—and she sniffled.

Fingers hovering over the keyboard, I sighed. "He can't do that, legally."

Her mouth twisted. "Maybe not, but nothing can be done about it. He knows how to work the system. He left the area and will probably find a job that pays in cash, so no one can track his income."

Was that what Stephen was doing to Julia? If he'd quit his job, and no one knew where he was… I didn't know what she got for child support, but he'd definitely made a lot more than she did. Then again, unlike Amber, Julia was better prepared for single parenthood.

Chapter 6

Julia

Just a little over a week before Thanksgiving, and Indian summer had made a comeback. One day it was drizzly and cool, and the next it was in the mid-seventies. What we needed was rain. That was the California resident's mantra. But as I drove through downtown during my lunch hour, rain didn't appear to be in today's forecast.

Margaret lived in a small house just off Schnell School Road in Placerville. She and Stephen's father had been divorced since he was in high school, and Stephen had rarely seen him since. I'd never met the man, but it didn't take a psychiatrist to see how an absentee father had led to Stephen's own paternal shortcomings. How could he model what he didn't know?

I parked in front of Margaret's house. Clean, tidy, and functional, with pots of orange chrysanthemums and purple pansies to welcome visitors to the porch. I climbed out of my car and hesitated. I could've just called, but I didn't want to have this conversation over the phone.

With each step toward the front door, my heartbeat escalated, and it became harder to breathe. Why did I feel like an insecure schoolgirl? Yes, things had been tense between us, but I should have pushed through it instead of letting it grow like an errant weed.

I pressed the doorbell with a trembling finger, crossed my arms, and waited. The door was solid, so other than the faint tread of footsteps, I had no warning before it was opened.

Margaret looked much like the last time I had seen her. Her thin face was framed by a salt-and-pepper bob that curved just below her chin. Maybe the lines around her gray eyes and mouth were a little more pronounced.

She gave a hesitant smile. "Julia. What are you doing here?"

"May I come in? We need to talk."

Her eyes widened as her mouth opened slightly, but she moved back so I could enter. "Is Max okay?"

Her concern over Max eased the tension in my shoulders. "He's doing well. Thanks for asking."

She led the way into the family room, where I noticed small changes. A new coffee table and a couple of potted plants. "Do you want something to drink?"

"Thanks, but no. I have to get back to work, so this will be quick." *I hope.*

With a wave of her hand, she invited me to sit on the sofa, while she eased into a faded wing-back chair. "If your visit isn't about Max, it must be about Stephen."

"Have you seen or spoken with him lately?"

She sat a little straighter. "Why? Is there something wrong?"

I sighed. "That's what I was hoping you could tell me. When was the last time you talked to him?"

"I don't know. It's been quite a few days. Maybe last week-end." She leaned forward. "What's going on, Julia?"

I rubbed my forehead. Now what? I was sure she'd know where Stephen was, I hadn't considered any other possibility.

"Saturday, Stephen told me he was moving to Arizona. Do you know anything about this?"

She shook her head. "I'm sure he won't make a move without talking to me." But her voice was weak, belying her confidence.

Never having been close to my mother-in-law, the sudden need to protect her feelings was as foreign to me as a pair of Jimmy Choo heels, and just as uncomfortable. "I'm sorry to be the bearer of bad news, but it appears he already has. Moved, I mean."

"I don't understand." She rose from the chair and stepped to the sliding glass doors that overlooked the backyard. It was as tidy and well kept as the front. She stood in a patch of sunlight and turned to me. "You don't think he'd just leave without telling us, do you?"

I shrugged. "It doesn't seem likely, but I don't know where he'd be otherwise. Every time I call, I get a message his voice-mail is full. So, yesterday morning I went to his apartment to talk to him, but he was already gone."

"This doesn't make any sense," she whispered, hugging her arms across her body. "Do you believe he's in some kind of trouble?"

"He hasn't been the most attentive of fathers, and God knows we've had our issues, but I wouldn't have expected him to run off like this."

She pinned me with sharp eyes. "Then you do think he's in trouble."

"I don't know, Margaret. I thought for sure he would have talked to you." I stood and rounded the coffee table to reach her side. I itched to hug her, but to do so might have made us both feel awkward. Instead, I stopped a couple feet from her. "It wasn't my intention to worry you. I'm sure he's just busy. I'll keep trying to reach him."

She nodded. "You'll let me know if you hear anything?"

"Of course. Will you do the same?"

"Yes." She touched trembling fingers to her lips, and her gray gaze met mine. "Would it be okay if I come by your place to see Max this weekend?"

Awkward or not, I couldn't help but wrap my arms around her.

Marty

I parked my Jeep at the curb and observed the house for signs of life. The porch light was on, as well as a soft glow coming from the front windows. It was after eight. Surely Julia hadn't gone to bed yet. Maybe I should have called. It was a rare thing for me to just drop in on her. We'd never had that kind of friendship. Now here I was, for the third time in three days, without a good excuse.

Sitting in my vehicle like a stalker was not my usual M.O. But then, neither was indecision. When Julia peered out the window, probably trying to decide whether to call the cops or not, I knew I was busted. I climbed out of the Jeep and waved at her.

She opened the front door before I reached the porch. "I thought that was you." She offered a soft smile.

I blurted the first thing I could think of. "I was in the neighborhood." Yeah, like she wasn't going to see right through that cliché line. But what did it matter? Playing it cool hadn't gotten me anywhere with her. Maybe it was time to up the stakes a bit.

"If you say so." She led the way inside. "I was just making a cup of tea. Would you like one?"

"Sure." I followed her into the kitchen. Except for the strains of a Christian rock song playing from her phone on the counter, the house was quiet. "Where's Max?"

"In bed, asleep." She filled a kettle with water and set it on the stove. "I have chamomile, peppermint, or black."

"Uh, whatever you're having."

She took a couple mugs and a box of tea from the cabinet. "Are you going to tell me why you're really here?"

The kitchen table sat in a small alcove overlooking the backyard, and I slipped into one of the four chairs surrounding it. "I just had a random thought earlier today."

She rested her hip against the counter and grinned at me. "Do you get many of those?"

"My fair share, I suppose."

"Does this random thought, perchance, have anything to do with me?" The kettle whistled, and she shut off the gas. Steam and the faint scent of peppermint rose from the mugs as she filled them.

"Just wondering how Stephen's disappearing act affects your child support payments."

She handed me a mug of tea and sat across from me with her own. "What brought this on?"

I slid the mug aside and looked across the table at her. "You know about my volunteering at the Urban Outreach."

"I've picked up a little here and there. What about it?"

"A meeting I had with a single mom today made me think of you. Her story sounds a little like yours. I've been trained to stick my nose in where it doesn't belong, so feel free to tell me if I'm overstepping."

She picked up her mug and blew into it before taking a tentative sip. Her cheeks were pink, probably from the steam. "You're fine. My finances could be a problem. I should have received a payment over the weekend."

"You still don't have any idea where he is?"

"No. I went by to see his mom today, but she doesn't know anything, either."

"What are you going to do?"

She wrapped her hands around the mug and shrugged. "What can I do?"

"You should tell your attorney, for one thing."

"The only attorney I know is the mediator we used for the divorce. But what good would it do to share this with him?"

"For one thing, he can make sure that if Stephen gets another job, child support payments will be attached to his wages." Unless he was going to pull what Amber's ex did and find a way around the system. That was a path I hoped Julia wouldn't have to travel. "If you need help with that, we have legal aid at the center, and I could connect you."

She rubbed a thumb along the rim of her cup. "I appreciate it. If I don't hear from Stephen in the next couple of days, I'll be sure and follow up on it." Her gaze slipped away from mine. "Is that all?"

I could formulate numbers in my head almost as quick as a calculator, but when it came to sharing my heart? Nothing computed. "Uh, yeah. I just wanted to make sure you're doing okay."

"We're doing fine." She fiddled with her tea bag. "How about you? I imagine you'll be starting on corporate taxes soon."

This was sad. Enough of the small talk. "Look, Jules." I reached across the table and touched her hand. "We've been dancing around this issue for months."

Mouth opened slightly, she blinked. "I'm not sure what you mean." Her gaze dropped to my hand still on hers, and she sat back, breaking the connection.

Great. Now I'd bumbled things. "Never mind." I slid the mug to the middle of the table. "Forget I said anything."

She blew out a sigh. "You've been such a good friend, Marty. I don't want to mess that up."

"Neither do I." I let my gaze rest on her soulful brown eyes. There was warmth and fear and indecision flickering in their depths. Maybe we weren't cut out for more than friendship. "It's fine, really. Whatever it is between us seems like it's been the elephant in the room lately, but if you're okay with the status quo, so am I. I'm here for you, regardless."

As I walked to the door, I gave myself a figurative head slap. I wouldn't win any awards for eloquence.

Chapter 7

Julia

Thanksgiving with the O'Shay's was an experience in tradition and inclusion. Anyone who was there, whether born an O'Shay or not, was considered family. It was the only time Sean cooked at the restaurant anymore. And although we each brought something to the table (apple crostata from me), the basics—turkey, dressing, mashed potatoes, and gravy—were Sean's domain. He said no one could make potatoes like an Irishman.

The restaurant was closed to patrons, and a couple tables were decked out in the middle of the dining room with white and gold linen tablecloths, tall orange tapers, and Thanksgiving-themed plates. Another table was set up for appetizers and drinks. Mouthwatering aromas wafted from the kitchen where Sean and Fiona attended to the finishing touches on the meal. Or so they said. But no one dared to interrupt the newlyweds to confirm that was true. Maris and Katie laid out the appetizers they'd made, while Tess and I set out plates and utensils.

I handed Max a stack of cloth napkins. "Put one on each plate, okay?"

Max asked the question I had been dying to. "Where's Marty?"

Tess attempted to ruffle his curls as he dodged her. "Believe it or not, he has his own family."

"Really?" He looked at her as if she'd said he had two heads. "I thought we were his family."

"Afraid not, kiddo."

Jake pushed through the swinging doors that separated the back of the building from the dining room. "Baby Sean's down." He held up a monitor. "I closed the door to Julia's office, but if he wakes, we'll hear him through this."

I stifled a grin. Jake the doctor and Jake the dad were not the same man. "Did you happen to check the kitchen to see how dinner's coming?"

He gave me a horrified grimace. "Not on your life. They're like a couple of high school kids."

Katie turned from her task. "I'll do it. It'll be payback for all the times Dad just happens to come into the family room when I'm hanging out with Tony. As if I don't know what he's doing." She popped a stuffed mushroom into her mouth and disappeared through the doors.

"Brave girl," Jake said.

Tess laughed. "She'll be sure to make enough noise to give them fair warning." She sidled up next to me, hands filled with spoons. "Are you okay?"

Heat flooded my cheeks. Of course, Tess would know something was off. Didn't she always? Although I tried to focus on the festivities, my mind was on Marty. It had been more than a week, and I couldn't shake our uneasy conversation. I glanced around to be sure no one was within hearing distance. "I think I hurt Marty's feelings."

She cocked her head. "How?"

"With my big mouth, that's how. He came over last week to find out if I'd heard from Stephen, and I might have said something stupid."

Tess patted my arm. "I'm sure it's not as bad as you think. What happened?"

"He said something about us dancing around our issue and it being an elephant in the room."

"Marty?" Her eyes widened.

"What about Marty?" Jake offered a plate of appetizers to each of us.

"It's nothing." Just what I needed—Jake privy to my pathetic, non-existent love life.

Tess raised an eyebrow at me—her nonverbal way of reminding me I could trust Jake.

I sighed. "He kind of implied that he has feelings for me, and I didn't handle it very well. We haven't talked since, and my stomach's in knots. I was hoping he'd be here tonight."

Tess put her free arm around me. "You know, Jules, you can always call him."

"I don't even know what to say."

"He'll be home from San Diego on Sunday," Jake said. "That gives you a few days to figure it out."

Tess waited until he left, then looked at me. "If my pushing you to give Marty a chance added to your confusion, I apologize. What I think doesn't matter. What do you want, Jules?"

Good question.

Throughout the evening, I thought about it. I'd always thought of Marty as Jake's fun sidekick. When did things shift between us? Since our stilted conversation the week before, my heart fluttered whenever I thought about him. I pictured the dimple in his chin and his crooked smile. But in the past, I'd gone through all the same emotions with Stephen, and the heartache wasn't worth the risk. Or was it?

Two hours later, Max and I got settled in the car, and I checked my phone. One text—from an unknown number. *In Glendale, AZ. All is fine. Tell Max hi.* I drew in a deep breath.

Stephen. The new number raised more questions, but at least I knew he was safe.

Christmas music played on the car radio, and I hummed along, my heart lighter than it had been since Stephen left.

"Are we almost home?" Max asked around a yawn. Too much excitement and more sugar in one night than he'd seen in a month had him ramped up like the Road Runner. Now he was dropping faster than Wile E. Coyote from a cliff.

"A few more minutes, kiddo." I checked the rearview mirror. The streets were empty, except for one car behind me. Had it been there since I left the restaurant? A shiver skittered up my spine. It was my imagination between Stephen's sudden disappearance, the strange visit from his supposed friend Glen, and late-night television crime dramas, a Lee Child novel would've put me right over the edge.

My phone rang through the car speakers like an air horn, and my heart leapt to my throat. When Margaret's caller ID appeared on the dashboard, I took a breath before connecting the call.

"Hello? Margaret?"

"Julia. Happy Thanksgiving. It sounds like you're in the car."

"I am. Can you hear me okay?"

"Is Max there?"

Max sat straight; energy temporarily restored. "Hi Grandma."

"Hello, sweet boy."

Although I'd asked her to join us tonight, she had declined.

"Julia, can you call me back when you get home? I need to talk to you about the situation we've been discussing."

"Has there been some communication?"

"Yes." The one word sounded stilted.

"On my end, as well. I'll call you as soon as I get Max down."

❆

Marty

It was hard to get into the spirit of the holidays when it was seventy-two and sunny outside. The smell of turkey roasting would help, but Dad was into deep frying. Sacrilegious. It was a small gathering—Mom, Dad, my sister Celia, her husband Tom, and their two kids, Michelle and T.J. Most everyone was out back watching the turkey fryer. Perfect for me since the food was in the kitchen.

Mom was at the counter arranging snacks on a platter. She slapped my hand when I reached for a slice of cheese. "I'm trying to make them look nice."

"That'll last about ten seconds, you know."

"Presentation is important."

I laid an arm across her shoulders, made a covert move for a slice of salami, and popped it into my mouth before she could stop me.

"Hey Marty." Celia came in from the dining room. "Could you get us another chair for the dining room table?"

"There are already seven."

"Well, we need eight."

"Here, Marty." Mom shoved the platter at me then shooed me with her hands. "Take this out back while we finish up in here."

Something smelled fishy, and it wasn't the smoked salmon. "Okay, who's coming that you don't want me to know about?"

"Don't look at me." Mom gave Celia's back a pointed look as my sister escaped to the dining room.

I left the platter on the counter and followed Celia. She was on the far side of the table squeezing in one more place setting.

"What'd you do, Sis?"

The doorbell rang. "I thought it would be nice to round

out the party a little." She flashed a smile over her shoulder while moving across the living room.

What was that supposed to mean? But it became clear as black ice when she opened the door and Gillian stepped in with a bottle of wine. I should have known. My stomach clenched, and it was everything I could do to keep the salami down. What could my little sister have been thinking?

"It's been a long time, Marty." Gillian turned her model-perfect smile on me, which had the opposite effect I was sure she was shooting for.

It was on the tip of my tongue to respond with a rude comeback, but Mom's eyes drilled into the back of my head, and I could almost hear her coaching me on manners. "Gillian, this is a surprise." It was the best I could do under the circumstances.

"Let's not stand in the doorway." Celia whisked Gillian into the room and closed the door behind her.

"So nice that you can join us, Gillian." Mom crossed the living room and gave her a quick hug. "The party's out back. Why don't we get you something to drink and join everyone?"

I looped Celia's arm with mine as she tried to pass me. "You two go ahead. Celia and I have a few more things to do in here."

Once out of earshot, I turned to her. "A little heads-up would have been nice."

Her smile wavered. "I ran into her the other day, and she asked about you. It's obvious she still has feelings for you. She's unattached. You're unattached. I thought it would be the perfect opportunity to see if the sparks are still there." She planted innocent eyes on me—the look she'd always used to wriggle out of trouble.

I held my hands up. "Oh, they're there all right, but not in a good way."

She winced. "I thought you moved north because you were so broken-hearted."

I snorted. "I wasn't broken-hearted, just broken. And I went up north to help out Gramps."

"I figured that was just an excuse." She dropped into a chair, propped her elbows on her knees, and looked up at me with sad eyes. "You don't have any feelings for her?"

I sat on the coffee table, our knees nearly bumping, and mirrored her posture. "Not unless disgust counts."

She scraped her hair back. "I'm so sorry, Marty."

"It's partly my fault," I said. "I never told you what happened between us, so you couldn't have known." Why would I want my little sister to know of my humiliation?

"So, what did happen?"

"Let's just say she liked to play the field."

"One of those, huh?"

"Afraid so."

She sighed. "Great. Now what do we do?"

I raised my eyebrows. "We?"

Scowling, she slapped my knee. "Oh, come on. You're not going to leave me to deal with this on my own, are you? What kind of a brother would do that?"

"You're right." I stood up. "I'll just tell her you made a mistake and ask her to leave."

Her eyes went wide. "You wouldn't dare."

"Relax." I patted her shoulder. "I'll be cool. But from now on, let me handle my own love life, will you?"

"What love life?" She grinned. "You're almost forty. It's about time you pull your own weight around here. I can't be the only one blessing the units with grandkids."

I grabbed her hand and tugged until she stood. With an arm around her shoulders, I walked her toward the backyard. "You never know. I might just surprise you some day."

Julia's face flashed in my mind. Unwise choices were made when I failed to pray, like with Gillian. The more I prayed for Julia, and about her, the more I felt she was God's choice for me. She just didn't know it yet. I needed to be patient enough to wait for His timing and not push before she was ready.

Chapter 8

Julia

In what seemed like the blink of an eye, Placerville's historic Main Street was transformed from a quaint old town to a picturesque Christmas scene. The fifty-foot bell tower was decked out with Christmas lights and wreaths. More beribboned greenery hung from the old-fashioned lamp posts that lined the sidewalks. Swags of pine boughs, colorful adornments, and enough bling to keep a Kardashian happy alighted shop windows and doorways.

Ever since I'd worked at Bella Cucina, the Monday after Thanksgiving had been set aside for decorating the restaurant. In light of our task, Maris piped Christmas music through the speakers. We'd unloaded boxes of ornaments, garlands, and twinkle lights, and it looked as if elves had bombed the dining room.

"Where do you want to start?" I held up a string of lights and glanced at Maris, while Dean Martin crooned about the delightful winter weather.

"With the tree, of course." A Santa-sized, red canvas bag sat like an inebriated sailor on a hand truck in the middle of the room. "Do you think we should put it in the same corner as last year?"

"Sure." It didn't really matter to me. If I was going to be any help at all, I needed to shake the cloud that loomed over me.

She held up a box of ornaments. "Do you want to trim the tree while I hang swags of garland?"

"Sounds good." I hummed harmony to Brenda Lee's "Rockin' Around the Christmas Tree," hoping it would infect me with a little seasonal joy.

I'd been wound up tighter than a toy top since Thursday night. A heaviness of foreboding made my chest tight. Every vehicle behind me was suspect. Twice, I'd seen someone just sitting in their car across the street from the house. I couldn't make out a face due to the glare of the late afternoon sun and the reflection of the trees on the windows.

The first time I noticed it, I didn't think anything of it. When it appeared again the following day, I noted the make, model and license plate and called the police. By the time the officer showed up, the car was gone. It's on record now, and a patrol car would be surveilling the area over the next few days. Still, it was unsettling.

"Earth to Julia," Maris singsonged, breaking into my one-woman paranoia party. She was standing near the top of a six-foot ladder, arms filled with fake garland. "Give me a hand, will you?"

"Oh, sorry." I maneuvered around storage boxes and tables oozing red and green glitz. I took the end of the garland in one hand as Maris hooked the other end on the wall.

Climbing down, she glanced at me. "Are you feeling all right? You're not your usual chatty self today."

"Just a little distracted."

"Have you heard from Stephen yet?"

"Yes, finally. He texted on Thursday night to tell me he's in Arizona. Nothing since then, but at least that's something."

"You haven't actually talked to him?"

"No, but at least I know where he is. Kind of."

She repositioned the ladder. "What're you going to do?"

I shrugged. "What can I do but wait it out?"

"You're such an innocent." She took the garland from me and stepped up to the ladder. "All you need is someone who's a little tech-savvy, and you can locate him by his phone number."

"You mean ping him?" Wasn't that the term I'd heard bandied about on police dramas?

"It's the same idea." With the garland hung over an arm, she climbed up the ladder. "Of course, it won't do you any good if you're not willing to go wherever he is and confront him."

I picked up a box of ornaments and hugged it to my chest. "Do I dare ask how you know this?"

She hung the end of the garland and descended the ladder. "I have a brother who's gone AWOL a time or two. As long as I know he's okay, I can sleep at night."

It took a moment for her words to penetrate. "I didn't know you have a brother."

"It's not common knowledge." She stepped off the last rung and turned to me. "It's hard to think about him some-times, let alone talk about him."

I was about to respond when a noise came from the back hallway. Someone was here. "Did you lock the door?"

Maris shook her head. "It's probably Sean."

"Probably." Still, my heartbeat kicked up a notch or two. What if it was that creep Glen? A sense of déja vu tapped at the recesses of my mind as if this very scenario was part of my late-night dreams.

"Anyone here?" The door swung open and Marty stepped

through. I blew out a breath, although my heart didn't settle. Was it because of how we had left things the last time we saw each other, or was it the dimple in his cheek and warmth in his eyes?

Marty

Gramps had been great with the sayings—*a Daniel come to judgment; turkeys voting for Christmas; neither a borrower nor a lender be; a change is as good as a rest.* Gramps—the wisest man I'd ever known—hadn't been a fan of Gillian's, but I would've bet every hair on my head he would have loved Julia.

Even though the restaurant was closed on Mondays, I knew Julia still worked in the office. No time like the present (another of Gramps' sayings) to put my plan into action. Rather than the quiet I expected when I opened the back door, I heard Burl Ives singing "Holly Jolly Christmas." Jules wasn't in her office, so I continued down the hall to the dining room and pushed through the partition. It looked as if someone had laid a Christmas bomb and left them with the fallout.

"Hey, you two."

Julia stepped across the sea of green and red toward me, a smile hovering on her lips.

"We weren't expecting you." She included Maris with a quick glance.

Maris grinned. "I doubt *we* are who he came to see."

I tucked my hands into the front pockets of my jeans. "Just thought I'd come by and see if you're free for lunch."

"Lunch?" The delight in her eyes was a dead giveaway. But then she did a quick scan of the dining room and frowned. She had the worst poker face I'd ever seen.

"Don't let this stop you." Maris waved at the mess. "We'll get it knocked out this afternoon with no problems."

"You're welcome to join us," I told her. "And I'd be happy to help out here for a couple hours afterwards. I have to be in Sacramento at four, but until then I'm all yours."

Maris smirked. "I have no desire to be a third wheel on your date."

Julia's cheeks turned pink. "It's not a date." She looked at me. "Right, Marty?"

"Call it whatever you want." *Slow and steady wins the race.* "Either way, you're welcome to come, Maris."

She folded the ladder and grinned at me over her shoulder. "I appreciate the offer, but I have plans. Just make sure you come back with her."

A few minutes later, we stepped into the alleyway. Unlike San Diego, the air was fall-crisp. "Are you up for walking down to Sweetie Pies?"

"I'm glad you stopped by." She touched my arm and glanced up at me. "It gives me a chance to apologize for our last conversation."

"You have nothing to apologize for. As long as we can remain friends, I'm happy." I'd leave God in charge of the details. "So, Sweetie Pies?"

"Sounds good."

"Are you going to be warm enough?"

"It's a five-minute walk."

I fell into step as she started down the alley. "So, anything new since we last talked?"

"If you mean have I heard from Stephen, then yes. A short text. He's in Arizona, like I suspected, but that's it. Maris was just telling me that I can find his location using his phone number." She hugged her sweater tighter around her body. "Have you ever heard of such a thing?"

We came out onto the sidewalk and had to wait for a couple cars to pass before we could cross the street. Once we were in the sunlight, the temperature rose, cutting through the chill. "No, but I'm not surprised. If you find him, then what?"

I itched to take her hand, but until she was ready to take the next step, I had no right.

"I haven't gotten that far yet." She loosened the hold on her sweater. "Enough about Stephen. How was your Thanksgiving?"

"Enlightening."

"Well, that sounds intriguing. Tell me more."

Slow and steady. "My sister blindsided me."

"You have a sister? Older or younger?"

I laughed. "You don't have to sound so shocked. It's not all that unusual. Celia is five years younger."

"Celia?" She nodded. "That's right. You've mentioned her before."

"I suppose we've rarely talked one-on-one. We're usually hanging out with Jake and Tess. I don't know much about your family either. Like, your parents."

She gave me a sideways glance. "I have two. A mom and a dad."

"Yeah? Do they live far away?"

"No. They're right here in town."

"Then why do you spend the holidays with the O'Shay's?"

"That's a little more complicated. I'd rather hear how your sister blindsided you."

"I think we should be sitting for this one." We arrived at Sweetie Pies, and I took her arm as we navigated around outside tables and chairs before climbing the wooden steps. I'd heard the Victorian house that now housed the restaurant was the oldest home on Main Street.

After we placed our order at the counter, we found a small table tucked away in a corner intimate enough for a private conversation.

Julia didn't waste any time on small talk. "Okay, we're seated. How did your sister blindside you?"

While pouring cream into my coffee, I took the opportunity to assess her. She was no Gillian, which was a huge plus.

Julia wore little makeup, as far as I could tell. Then again, Celia was always telling me I was clueless when it came to that kind of thing. But there didn't seem to be any artifice to her— what you saw was what you got. It was refreshing.

Julia arched her eyebrows. "You're stalling."

I took a sip of coffee. "You seem awfully eager."

A smile flirted around the corners of her mouth. "You have me curious, is all."

"Well, before I moved to Placerville, I was in a long-term relationship with a woman named Gillian."

She looked down and swiped at the condensation on her glass of iced tea.

"Celia invited her to Thanksgiving without telling me."

"Oh?" Her eyes flicked toward me and back down again. "Was that a good thing or a bad thing?"

I kept a laser focus on Julia to discern her reaction. "Definitely a good thing."

Her shoulders dipped by the slightest degree. "That's… great." There was a catch in her voice. She cleared her throat and turned her gaze toward me, eyes not quite meeting mine. Her words about just being friends didn't match her body language.

"I think so. I mean, even though I was hurt and angry with her when I broke it off, I wondered if there were still feelings lurking in the background."

She tilted her head "And?"

"Not a one." I propped my elbows on the table and leaned toward her. "So, I have a question for you."

"What's that?"

"Do you still have feelings for Stephen?"

"I have all sorts of feelings for him: irritation, frustration, betrayal. Take your pick."

Life just got a little more interesting.

Chapter 9

Julia

Tourists flocked to Placerville during the Christmas season to experience the small-town holiday festivities—maybe to get a glimpse of what inspired Thomas Kinkade. They came from as far as the Bay Area or as close as Sacramento and kept the restaurants and small businesses hopping. It was a good thing for the economy. Not so good for those of us with young children who had an agenda.

The line to visit Santa was ridiculous, but Max insisted. I was pretty sure he'd known for the last two years who Santa was. Or wasn't. Either way, I was aware Santa visits were how he used his little boy wiles to clue me in to what he wanted for Christmas. It wasn't quite manipulation, but close enough.

Marty took one look at the queue and balked. "How 'bout I get us some hot chocolate?"

Max's eyes widened. "I want chocolate."

I gave him "The Look" honed by years of parenting.

"Please?" he translated.

I ruffled his hair. *Good boy.* "That's sweet of you, Marty, but completely unnecessary."

"Hey, I'm here to serve."

I watched the back of his blond head until he was swallowed by the crowd. How had we gotten here? Somewhere between our bumbling conversation about staying friends and lunch at Sweetie Pies, something had shifted. It wasn't anything I could point to—nothing tangible—just slight nuances. A look, a smile, an expression.

"This is taking for*ever.*" Max peered around the snail's-pace line. "Are we gonna miss the light parade?"

I pushed my coat sleeve back with a gloved hand and checked my watch. "How important is it that you see Santa?"

He pursed his lips and squinted at me. "I guess I can write him a letter."

"A letter, huh?" If he believed in Santa, then that ought to suffice. But if he didn't—

"And you can check it for mistakes before I send it. Just in case."

There it was. The catch. As long as I read it, he figured I'd know what to get him from Santa. "Let's step out of line, Max, and talk about it." There was no way I was going to discuss this around little believing ears.

We squeezed through a group of people and found an opening large enough for the two of us against a gift shop window.

"Okay, kiddo, let's have a little heart-to-heart."

Max tilted his head back to look at me, his nose scrunched up. "What's that?"

"It's where we're completely honest with each other. Deal?"

He sighed. "I guess."

"What do you know about Santa?"

"Well, he lives in the North Pole with a bunch of elves and rides in a sleigh on Christmas Eve."

I arched my brows. "You *know* this?"

"And if I don't believe in him, then I don't get Christmas presents."

I cupped his cheek in my gloved hand. "I think you have Santa mixed up with Jesus. Believing in Santa doesn't get you anything. But believing in Jesus gets you into heaven."

Marty appeared, a Styrofoam cup in each hand. "You didn't already see the big guy, did you?"

"No. We're debating the whole Santa scene." I took a sip of the hot chocolate. Lukewarm and instant. Definitely unworthy of the name. "Where's yours?"

Marty jammed his hands into his coat pockets. "I think I'll hold out for coffee." He looked at Max who now had a chocolate mustache.

"What's a debate?" Max took another gulp of the drink. It was a good thing it wasn't actually hot, or he'd have had a scalded tongue.

Marty pulled a hand from his pocket and rubbed his chin. "Well, it's kind of like a discussion between two people who have different points of view. Like, maybe you believe in Santa and your mom doesn't. Or your mom believes in Santa, but you don't."

Max scrunched up his nose. "I don't think Mom believes in Santa." He turned his gaze on me. "Do you, Mom?"

Talk about a rock and a hard place. "It's not important what I believe. I want to know what you believe."

"Well." He swiped at his upper lip. "As long as I get presents either way."

I nudged him with my elbow. "That's what I thought." I could only hope he didn't ask for anything outside my limited budget. Stephen always came through with the extravagant guilt gifts.

"The Festival of Lights starts in about a half hour." Marty scanned the crowd. "Not that we'll see anything with all these people here."

"I may not have a Park Avenue view like the mom in

Miracle on 34th Street, but this isn't the Macy's Thanksgiving Day Parade, either."

"What're you talking about?"

I slipped my arm through his. "Come with me."

One of the perks of working for Sean O'Shay was having access to the storeroom above the restaurant, with windows looking down on Main Street. The perfect place to watch the parade in relative comfort and peace. By the time it was over, Max was curled up in a blanket on the floor, and my legs had fallen asleep from sitting in a cheap lawn chair. Maybe it was time to invest in some decent parade-viewing furniture.

"I guess he came down from his sugar high." Marty bent over to pick him up.

"Oh, Marty, don't do that. He can walk."

"It's no problem." He carried him through the storeroom and down the stairs as if he weighed no more than a sack of sugar.

Max didn't make a sound until Marty pulled his Jeep into my driveway. "Where are we?"

"Home, sweetie. You missed most of the parade."

"Aww, *man.*"

Unbuckling my seatbelt, I glanced at the house. Was that a light glowing from somewhere in the back? My stomach lurched as though I was about to drop from the top of a roller coaster. I hadn't left any lights on.

"Jules? Are you okay?" Marty touched my arm.

I shifted to see Max. "Stay here, okay?"

"Why?" Max scrambled forward and peered through the windshield.

"Because I said so." Even he knew not to argue with such an illogical comeback.

Once out of the Jeep, I pulled Marty aside. "I think someone's in my house. Or was in my house."

"What?" Marty's face was shadowed, but the snap of his one-word question left no doubt he was on full alert. "Why?"

"There's a light on." I peered at the living room window. "I think it's in the kitchen."

"Maybe you left it on."

I shook my head. "I didn't. I never leave lights on." No need for him to know that I was pinching every penny I could.

"Give me your keys. I'll go check it out."

I clutched his arm. "What if he's still here? Shouldn't we call the police?"

"I'm just going to take a quick look."

I imagined Marty getting hit on the head or worse. "It could be dangerous."

"Get back in the Jeep, lock the doors, and have your phone handy."

"This isn't a good idea," I said. But I gave him my keys and climbed back in the Jeep anyway.

Max's head popped between the front seats. "What's he doing?"

"Nothing for you to worry about, sweetie." I watched as a hunched Marty skulked down the side of the house and disappeared behind the back gate while I pulled out my phone and called the police. Marty may need to play the hero, but I wasn't taking any chances.

"9-1-1. What's your emergency?"

After reporting the break-in, I stayed on the line as instructed. I was reminded of a scene from *To Kill a Mockingbird* where Jem told Scout to stay put and count to ten while he snuck back into the neighbor's yard for something he forgot. His pants, maybe? My eyes burned from the unblinking stare at the back gate, heart beating clear into my throat, while I counted to ten. Then again. Then once more before Marty reappeared, walking as if he hadn't a care in the world.

I jumped out of the Jeep and met him halfway. "Well?"

"You're either the world's lousiest housekeeper, or someone's trashed the place. We need to call the police."

I held the phone aloft. "They're on their way."

※

Marty

Max zonked out in the back seat before we left Placerville city limits. Fifteen minutes later, as we crossed the bridge onto my property, it was near midnight. It was during the police interview at Julia's house that I'd learned of her stalker. There was no way I was going to leave her and Max at the house right after a break-in, nor did any of us have energy to start the cleanup process yet. That could wait until the morning.

Julia peered out the window where towering pines shadowed the road as I drove the last quarter mile to the house. This wasn't the way I'd intended to show her the place. I couldn't attest to its cleanliness. Although, if I remembered correctly, I had picked up my breakfast dishes. That was something.

I parked outside the garage, turned off the ignition, and gazed at Julia. Moonlight danced off her dark hair and bathed her pale features. "Are you doing okay?"

She rubbed her face with both hands then pushed her hair back. "I've been asked that question more in the last couple weeks than the previous year."

"You've been through a lot."

"Still. I don't want to put anyone out. I could have called my parents."

"Why get them out of bed in the middle of the night? I have plenty of room."

"So I see." She unlatched the seatbelt and scooted forward to look out the windshield, although there wasn't much to see in the dark. I'd forgotten to turn on the outside lights when I left. "When you insisted we come home with you, I never expected it to be like this."

"What do you mean?"

"I don't know. I figured you lived in a small apartment

somewhere in town. Not a big house out in the country. And off Apple Hill Drive, of all places."

"Well, there's no point sitting out here. Might as well go inside and get you two settled." I hit the button attached to the sun visor to open the door and pulled into the garage.

"Will wonders never cease," Julia said. "You have a truck."

"So?"

"I would have expected a double slug bug with surfing equipment strapped to the roof." Laughter followed. She couldn't be in too bad of shape if she still had a sense of humor.

"You think I look like a surfer?"

"Kind of, yeah."

"Hate to disappoint you, but I've never surfed in my life. Now windsurfing? That's another thing altogether."

I carried Max through the house and up the stairs, turning on lights along the way, while Julia followed with a couple of small bags. The first bedroom down the hall was the one I had slept in when I used to visit Gram and Gramps. It looked much the same as it did when I had been Max's age. Lots of blue and red.

"Max should be comfortable in here."

Julia passed me and pulled down the bedspread and blankets. "Are you kidding? He may never want to leave. You'd tell me if you have a son, right?"

I chuckled. "This used to be my room." I laid Max's dead weight on the bed.

Julia bent over him and tugged off his shoes. "I thought you grew up in San Diego."

"I did. But my grandparents retired here when I was younger than Max. Every summer I spent my days fishing in the creek and living off the land."

"You lived off the land?" She wasn't buying it.

"Okay, so I exaggerated a little. Gramps grew his own vegetables. Gram had a bumper crop of blueberries and strawberries every summer. There's a pear orchard on the backside of the property and some other fruit trees in the garden."

Her eyes widened. "You're a farmer in your spare time?"

"Afraid not. It's more work than I can handle. The pear orchard still stands, and I keep the fruit trees trimmed, but other than that things grow wild." I shrugged.

"Still. You certainly surprise me."

"Yeah? Is that a good thing or a bad thing?"

She tucked a strand of hair behind her ear. "It's a good thing. Definitely."

I nodded. "You must be exhausted."

"One would think. I suppose all the excitement gave me a second wind."

"Let's go see if we can rustle up some real hot chocolate. It might be just what you need to sleep. And you'll need it staying in Celia's old bubble gum pink room."

I led the way back downstairs. A cursory glance at the kitchen confirmed that I'd remembered the breakfast dishes.

"Have a seat." I pulled out a stool from beneath the breakfast bar. "I'll make you the best cup of hot cocoa you've ever had."

Julia plopped onto the stool. "That's a pretty bold claim."

"You'll see." I rummaged in the cabinet until I found cocoa powder, sugar, a package of chocolate chips, and vanilla. A half-gallon container of milk and a can of whipped cream from the fridge, and I was ready to make good on my promise.

"You're serious."

"As a heart attack." I measured out two cups of milk, poured it into a pan and put it on the stove. "Which is what you'll have if you drink this on a regular basis."

She swiveled on the stool. "Your house is sadly lacking holiday spirit."

"It seems kind of pointless to decorate for myself, but what's your excuse? I already brought you a tree."

She wrinkled her nose. "Max and I have a tradition. We decorate a couple weeks before Christmas, and then leave everything up until after New Year's. But if I had a house like this, I'd deck the halls. Then I'd have a Christmas party and invite all my friends."

"*Mi casa es su casa.*"

"Yeah?"

I held up a wooden spoon. "Have at it."

Her smile faded. "I don't know what to do about this mess with Stephen. The only reason I can think of for someone to break in and not take anything is if they're looking for him."

"You should have said something before, Jules."

She swiped at her bangs. "I figured everyone would think I was paranoid."

If I'd had my way, Stephen would've moved to Timbuktu, never to be heard from again. But that wouldn't be fair to Max.

"What do you think I should do?" Her eyes pleaded for an answer.

"I think you should confront Stephen."

She scowled. "I have to find him first. Before whoever's after him does."

"Then let's do it."

Her eyes widened. "What?"

"I'll help you." Until she could put this mess to bed, she'd never be free of him.

Chapter 10

Julia

A ray of early morning sunshine lit the bedroom, and for a terrifying moment, I thought my nightmare of drowning in a bottle of Pepto-Bismol had come true. It wouldn't have been any more bizarre than the circumstances that had me sleeping in Marty's house. I blinked sleep from my eyes and pushed the pink and white coverlet aside. After a quick trip to the Jack and Jill bathroom (and a peek at Max sleeping on the other side), I got dressed. I needed a little fresh air and some perspective.

It was just after dawn, and with the late night we'd had, I suspected Marty was still sleeping. He'd told me last night that the master bedroom was on the first floor, so I tiptoed down the stairs. If I could score just a few minutes alone, maybe I could glean some godly words of wisdom. My jacket was slung over the couch, and I nabbed it on my way to the front door.

The cool air outside was replete with the sharp tang of pine. I closed my eyes and drew in a deep, cleansing breath. *Is there anything more resplendent than your creations, Lord?* Images from last night flitted through my mind—dresser drawers emptied on the floor, couch cushions upended, cabinets emptied. My heart rate increased with each one until my eyes snapped open. I would have a mess on my hands when I got home.

Zipping my jacket, I wandered around to the back of the house. A flagstone pathway cut through the lawn where railroad tie steps led down to a large fenced garden. I made my way to the wooden gate and unhooked the latch. Aside from scraggly weeds, the six raised beds sat empty among a variety of fruit trees. Two of them were bursting with apples, but the other three were bare.

I plucked an apple hanging on a low branch and inspected it. Not perfect like those found in the grocery store. Instead, it was smaller and slightly misshapen—the stem sitting at an odd angle like the eyes in a Picasso painting. I held it to my nose and drew in the sweet apple scent before biting into it. Sweet flavor burst on my tongue as juice dribbled down my chin. Perfect.

It was a reminder that no matter how messed up things got, I could always choose gratitude. I finished the apple and tossed the core for the birds.

What would you have me do, Lord?

There was a part of me that wanted to forget about Stephen. What did I care if he'd gotten himself into trouble? It wasn't like Max would miss him much. Stephen had been a haphazard father at best. But Max still needed him in his life. My own parents wouldn't have won any awards, but that didn't change that deep-down desire for their approval.

Honor thy mother and father.

"Good morning."

I spun around to find Marty carrying a steaming white mug in each hand. His hair was tousled, and the blond stubble on his cheeks and chin were more pronounced than usual. He'd never looked more like the surfer boy I'd accused him of being.

"Hope you like coffee. I don't have tea."

"I'll take what I can get."

"Cream or no cream?"

"Cream." He handed me one, and I wrapped my hands around the heat and inhaled the rich scent. "What would you have done if I said no cream?"

"I would've given you the other one. I'm good either way. Sugar?" He pulled a small brown packet from his jacket pocket.

Grinning, I took the packet from him. "You're a full-service host. Smells good."

"Peet's."

"Aren't you the coffee connoisseur?" I took a sip and savored the flavor. "Much better than the instant I drink at home."

He made a sour face. "Instant? Yuck. A chef like you ought to know better."

I laughed. "You look like Max when I try to get him to eat Brussels sprouts." I took in the view. "This is quite the place."

"I love it. My best childhood memories were made on these fourteen acres."

"How did you end up living here?"

"My grandmother died about three years ago from cancer." He frowned. "It seemed like Gramps gave up the will to live."

"So, you moved in?"

He nodded. "The timing was perfect, as it always is. I had just broken things off with Gillian, and I needed some distance. It was a win-win."

I pondered his words. "You said timing is always perfect. What did you mean by that?" His answer might give me the insight into his heart that I needed. We'd never discussed our faith with each other, but if I was going to trust him, this would be a key component.

Eyes meeting mine, he took a moment to drink his coffee.

"I believe everything happens in God's time. If I'd been better at waiting for that than rushing ahead of Him, like with Gillian, I could have saved a lot of heartache."

"You and me both." Had I trusted God, I would have never married Stephen. But then I wouldn't have Max, either. "Isn't it amazing, though, how He blesses us anyway?"

He nodded. "We wouldn't be standing here now." He brushed a strand of hair off my face. "Although I've been slow to admit it to myself, it's always felt like there was more at stake than friendship with you."

His admission left me breathless. Was this to be a pivotal conversation that could change everything? Did I want it to? The sudden lightness in my spirit told me I did. "So, where does that leave us?"

"Let's take it one step at a time. First you need to decide what to do about Stephen."

Marty

I made a quick phone call, and then Julia and I spent the better part of two hours putting her house back in order. It didn't seem to faze Max, for which we were grateful. When we were done, Julia dropped Max off at his grandma's, and the drive to El Dorado Hills took less than half an hour. Jerry, a *compadre* from the Urban Outreach, had been thrilled when I'd called him for his tech services. I'd lost count of the number of times he'd told me to call if I needed anything. I just didn't expect the day would come. We'd agreed to meet at Peet's Coffee at three.

The coffee house was packed—not unexpected on a Saturday during the holidays. Patrons surrounded the tables, some with laptops open, others laughing over a cup of their caffeinated beverage of choice. I could've used one of my own, but the line was too long. I spotted an empty table jammed into the corner, and we nabbed it. There wasn't enough space to breathe, let alone move around. But unless we wanted to sit outside, there was nothing to be done about it.

Julia shrugged out of her coat. "You're sure we can't get into trouble doing this? It can't be completely legal."

"It's not like you're doing it to hurt Stephen. How many messages have you left him since you received that one brief text from him?"

"It feels like a hundred."

"How else can you put this behind you if you aren't given the opportunity for a face-to-face? Your motives are pure, Jules."

"Mostly," she said. Her gaze was glued to the door, fingers tapping the table.

I placed my hand over hers. "Relax. It'll be fine." I sensed things were shifting for us, and I'd do whatever I could, within reason, to help Julia. Once the holidays were over, my life wouldn't be my own until the end of tax season. It was now or never.

She took a deep breath and turned to me with a weak smile. "Sorry. I've led a pretty clandestine-free life up until now. The last time I did anything sneaky was when I listened to a message on Stephen's phone. That's how I found out he was cheating on me."

"Fun times."

She hooked a strand of hair behind her ear. "I'm going to sound like a horrible person for admitting this, but there's a part of me that was relieved when Stephen said he was moving away. No more dealing with him. No more making excuses to Max when he bails on his weekends with him. How easy would it be to forget he existed, aside from the child support?" She gave me a sad smile. "Pathetic, huh?"

"Not at all. It's honest. Can't say I blame you." I touched

her hand. "But if that's how you feel, why even look for him? I'm sure with your skills, you'd be fine financially."

"True. But I realized it wouldn't be fair to Max. How would he feel if he finds out someday that I didn't fight for him? Or that I didn't care enough about his dad to try and find out what kind of trouble he's in? It might sound selfish, but I don't want this to come back on me."

I shook my head. "It doesn't sound selfish at all, Jules. Besides, Stephen has some explaining to do about this Glen character and the danger he put you two in."

I glanced toward the door and saw Jerry lumber in. He spotted me before I could raise a hand and maneuvered his large body around chairs and tables until he reached our corner.

Standing, I grasped his hand. "Thanks again for meeting us, Jer."

"Are you kidding? It's the least I can do after everything you do for us at the outreach." He pulled a chair out and plopped onto it, his large body dwarfing it. "You must be Julia." He stuck out his hand.

"Yes. I appreciate your help."

He dismissed it with a wave. "Happy to do it. So, I understand you have a missing husband."

"Ex-husband," Julia said. "The last I heard from him, he said he was in Glendale, Arizona."

"You have his phone number, I assume." He reached out, palm up.

A wrinkle formed between Julia's brows. "Uh, yeah."

"He wants your phone, Jules."

Her eyes widened. "Oh, of course." She pushed her chair back slightly to get access to the purse on her lap and combed through it. "Here it is." She swiped it open and handed it to him. "Let me write his number down for you."

Jerry rested his elbows on the table, the phone between his hands. "Is it in your contacts?"

"Yes. Stephen Metcalf."

He nodded then thumbed through it. After a few moments, he put it on the table and took his own from his jacket pocket.

Julia looked at me, eyebrows raised, and I shrugged. This was as much out of my wheelhouse as it was hers. I just happened to know the right people.

"Okay, got it." Jerry slid Julia's phone back to her. "I plugged his number into my app. Now we wait." He laid his phone on the table and watched it like it was going to perform a magic trick.

"I have a question for you, Jerry," Julia said.

"Ask away."

"If you can track this number, so can anyone else, right?"

"Anyone who has it and has received communication from it can."

I touched Julia's hand. "You're thinking of Glen?"

"Yes. But that doesn't seem likely."

"While we wait, anyone want something to drink?" I looked from Jerry to Julia.

"Black coffee for me," Jer said.

Julia jumped up. "Let me get it. It's the least I can do."

I gave her my order and watched until she turned the corner to the counter. "You do this often?"

He looked at me with a blank expression.

I pointed to the phone. "Track people."

Comprehension dawned, and he grinned. "A time or two. There are a lot of deadbeat dads out there. I make it my mission to equalize the bar a little when I can."

"Is it legal?"

He sucked air through his teeth and grimaced. "Legal. Illegal. There's a fine line between protecting a person's privacy and making them accountable." He shrugged. "What're you gonna do? Am I right?"

I pleaded the fifth.

He looked at the phone. "Bingo. Houston, we have a connection. Julia's information was right. The guy's in Glendale, Arizona." He used his fingers to zoom in on the screen. "Looks like a motel on North West Grand Avenue." He shifted it so I could see. "Isn't technology great?"

"As long as no one's using it on me."

"The thing is, when you get there, you'll probably want to plug his number in again to be sure he hasn't left."

When we get there? I hadn't thought that far in advance.

Chapter 11

Julia

Arms filled with a box of food, I knocked on Tess's kitchen door with the toe of my boot. The box got heavier by the second, and my nerves were frayed by dreams of espionage and clandestine meetings with a faceless man—as if I didn't know it was Stephen behind the void. A gust of wind sent a chill up my spine, and I shifted the box.

Footsteps and Tess's muffled voice reached me. "I'm coming." The door flew open, and a haggard Tess swept her arm in welcome. "My fairy godmother."

"This is getting heavy, and I'm freezing my hiney off out here." I slipped past her and slid the food onto the kitchen table.

"Ooh. What did you bring me?" She followed in my wake like a hungry puppy and peered around me into the box.

If Tess didn't have friends and family cooking for her, she and Jake would starve. Somehow, the culinary gene skipped her entirely. It was proof that the way to a man's heart was most definitely not through his stomach. At least not where Jake was concerned.

"Sustenance. You look like you could use it." I used both hands to retrieve a plastic gallon container. "Cioppino. Even after we eat lunch, there should be enough left over to feed you and Jake for a couple nights." I set it on the table and reached back in for a paper-wrapped loaf. "Sourdough French bread." My stomach rumbled as I inhaled the yeasty scent before placing it with the stew. Nothing settled frayed nerves better than a piece of sourdough slathered in real butter. "A Caesar salad and some cannoli."

"Wow." Tess fingered the white sack of cannoli. "How am I supposed to lose the baby weight eating like this?"

"Don't ask me." I slapped my hip. "I have a few post-pregnancy pounds of my own to lose."

She chuckled and rubbed her face. "I can see you're going to be a good influence on me."

"You look as exhausted as I feel. Is Sean keeping you awake at night?"

"I think he has his nights and days mixed up."

I sat across from her. "You need to sleep when he's asleep."

"I'll do that. *After* we eat." She stood and reached for the soup container.

"Allow me. You sit and rest."

I had the stew heating on the stovetop in record time. As I wrapped the bread in foil and put it into the oven, I noticed Tess's eyelids drooping. If I slipped out the door, she would be asleep before I could reach my car.

She straightened and shook her head as if trying to wake herself up. "Goodness, I had no idea having a baby could be so tiring."

I smiled. "You ain't seen nothin' yet, my friend. Wait until Sean's crawling. You'll be chasing him all over the place."

"So, we both know why I look like death warmed over. What's your excuse? Are you still worrying over the break-in?"

"Yes and no. I mean, the likelihood of it happening again

is pretty slim. The police are patrolling the area, and they have his vehicle information. But it motivated me to confront Stephen." I leaned against the counter.

She blinked. "How do you propose to do that?"

"Thanks to Marty, I know where he is."

Her eyebrows shot up. "Marty? Is there something going on between you two?"

"You mean other than friendship?"

She crossed her arms and stared at me as if she could mind-meld me. The thing is, she could.

"Okay, I don't know." I turned my attention to the stew, now bubbling in the pot. One more quick stir, and I turned off the gas. "Right now, I have to focus on this mess with Stephen. Then, *maybe*, I can think beyond a day or two."

"How did Marty find him?"

"A friend of his knew how to track him with his cell number. Anyway, he's in Glendale, Arizona. We're going to drive—"

"We?" She crossed her legs. "You mean you and Marty?"

I scowled at her. "Why do you say it like that?"

"I don't know. Maybe it's because a few weeks ago, you weren't willing to give him a chance. Now, he's the Jonathan to your David. Or should I say the Boaz to your Ruth?" She smirked.

"Your sense of humor deteriorates when you don't get enough sleep."

"Sorry. You're right. I just think you two would be great together. And it's not like you didn't constantly harass me about Jake."

She had a point. "Anyway, Marty offered to drive down with me. If I were the independent woman I claim to be, I'd go alone."

"I wouldn't let you." She crossed the kitchen and retrieved a couple bowls and salad plates from the cupboard. "I'd go if I could."

"I know you would. You have more important things to attend to here. Besides, having a little muscle could be helpful."

"What about Max?" She lifted the lid off the cioppino and inhaled. "We could take care of him."

"Your plate's full enough with baby Sean. Besides, Margaret offered, and I think it'll be good for both to spend time together." I ladled stew into the bowls.

"Strange how life turns out, isn't it?"

"What do you mean?"

She crossed the kitchen with the wrapped bread, a butter dish in her other hand. "Stephen isn't who you thought him to be. With him taking off like he did, your relationship with Margaret has gotten better, and then there's Marty. Before this happened, you two never spent any time alone. In the span of a few weeks, everything's shifted. No one is turning out to be who you thought them to be. It just goes to show you." She opened the salad container.

I placed the bowls of hot stew on the table and sat across from her. She was right. One way or another, I had misjudged them all. Could I have been just as shortsighted where my own parents were concerned?

It took almost an hour to find the shoebox full of photos in the back of my closet. I had come across one abandoned project after another—a partially knitted sweater, fabric from pillows I'd meant to sew, jeans that needed patching. All the things I enjoyed doing, but never seemed to find time for.

Once I retrieved the box of photos, it took another thirty minutes to comb through it. Every time I came across an interesting picture, I got lost wandering down memory lane. Who knew I'd ever need a real photo of Stephen? There was a five-by-seven of him with Max hanging in the hallway, but it would be better if I could find a smaller one of him. Everything being digital, photos were a rare thing these days. And the moment I had signed the were would have been that easy to erase him from my life.

The snapshot I found of him was years old, but good enough for identification. Aside from that, I found a couple photos of my parents—one with the three of us at a family reunion when I was a teenager and another of them taken at a studio more recently. They were posed and smiling in front of a blue background. I left all three photos, along with the box, on the coffee table when I stepped into the kitchen to prepare dinner.

"Hey, Mom?" Max wandered into the kitchen, one of the photos in his hand. "Who's this with Grandma and Grandpa?"

I didn't have to look at it to know which one he had. "That's me."

He squinted at it. "You look a lot younger with your hair really long."

I laughed. "It's not the hair, kiddo. That picture was taken years ago. I think I was in high school."

He wandered to the table, his eyes still on the photo. "How come we hardly ever see them?"

There was no way to explain disappointment to an eight-year-old. None that made sense, anyway. "I guess I'm not very close to them." Was that how Max would explain his relationship with Stephen one day?

"How come?"

I turned the burner down to simmer and joined him at the table. "It's one of those grown-up things that are hard to explain." It was ironic, really. They blamed me for Stephen's affair—if I'd just let this whole Jesus-freak thing go, then Stephen might not have felt the need to wander. At least from their perspective. My relationship with Jesus had intimidated him. Then again, I'd struggled with the divorce *because* of my relationship with Jesus. It was one thing to let down my parents. It was another to let down God.

"Don't you love them?"

I had to swallow a couple of times before I could find my voice. "Of course I love them." The question I struggled with was did they love me? In that moment, it occurred to me that I wasn't going to find the answer by shutting them out of my life. "How about this?" I folded my hands on the table and leaned toward him. "When I get back from Arizona, we'll go see them. Would you like that?"

He shrugged. "I guess." He handed me the photo. "I don't really know them."

An ache settled in my chest. "That's my fault. Once you spend a little time with them, you'll love them." From my lips to God's ear. "It didn't take you long to get close to Gigi, did it?" Margaret had asked Max to call her that, and he'd been only too happy to comply.

He grinned. "She's cool."

That was a word describing Margaret I'd never thought I'd hear. If Stephen's disappearing act did nothing else, it had brought us both closer to his mother. "Yes, she is. And you need to be on your best behavior while you stay with her."

His grin wavered. "Can't I go with you to see Dad? I'll be good, I promise."

"Not this time, sweetie. He's not really settled yet. Besides, Gigi's got all kinds of great plans for the two of you. I think she's going to take you to the hay and carriage rides on Friday night. And she talked about going to a movie. You don't want to miss those."

I held my breath as I waited for his response. A disappointed Max would be much harder to leave behind than a happy one.

"Okay. But you're gonna be home on Saturday, right?"

"Yes. And we'll get our tree on Sunday after church so we can decorate it."

His eyes lit up. "We already got the tree I picked out with Marty."

The tree that sat in Max's bedroom. "That one's for you, sweetie. We'll put lights and decorations on it, so you have something special all your own. But we need a big tree to put in the family room where everyone can see it."

"Yeah. It'll be great."

"Once we finish dinner, we'll get your stuff together and take you over. You'll spend three nights with her, okay?"

"Okay." Then his eyes widened. "I have to get my Game Box. I'm gonna teach Gigi how to play." He hopped off the chair and raced out of the kitchen.

There was the Max I knew and loved.

Even so, dread sat in the pit of my stomach. Was I making the right choice? Leaving Max for three nights was hard enough, but what if it didn't pan out? Or what if Stephen was doing something that went deeper than I was prepared to handle? And then there was Marty. This wasn't his problem, but he was certainly taking it on like it was.

Saturday night couldn't come fast enough for me.

Chapter 12

Marty

I'd always loved road trips. Driving to San Diego and back to visit my family was never a burden. Sure, I could've flown it in less time, but where would the fun be in that? Crowded airports, flight delays, dealing with a car rental never made flying worth it to me.

I pulled into Julia's driveway at three a.m. The street was dead quiet—no suspicious vehicles lurking in the neighborhood. The twinkle of Christmas lights outlined most of the neighbors' houses. Julia had a lot of nerve getting on me about my lack of Christmas spirit when her place was in the same deplorable condition.

The porch light was on, as well as the glow of a lamp through the front window, but no tree and no decorations. Did she at least put up the tree I'd bought for her at Apple Hill?

A true test of one's character was their mood in the wee hours of the morning. I was betting Jules believed there were better things to do this time of night—like sleep. Can't say I blamed her, but there was a method to my madness. If we left now, we would avoid Sacramento commute traffic, hit SoCal by mid-day, and be in Glendale by late afternoon.

I saw movement in the house as I ambled up the walkway. Julia had the door open before my foot hit the first step. She was wearing a thick sweater, stretchy black pants, and—*are those bunny slippers?* Her hair was piled in a knot, and her eyes were mere slits.

"Morning, sunshine." I stepped into the house and spotted her overnight case sitting on the coffee table. I glanced around for the tree, but it wasn't there.

She laid her head against the edge of the door as if she couldn't hold it up on her own. "There's something sick about a person who can be this cheerful in the middle of the night."

"Middle of the night? That boat sailed hours ago." I pointed to her bag. "Is that it, or do you have more?"

"Just my coat." She yawned. "And my tea."

While she gathered her things, I double-checked to be sure the house was locked, which was when I spotted the untransformed tree in Max's bedroom, and picked up her bag on my way to the front door. Her keys dangled from the lock, and she was already sitting in the Jeep—probably sound asleep. This was sure to be an entertaining drive.

Julia didn't make a peep until we hit I-5 in Sacramento. She stretched and yawned before speaking. "Where are we?"

"Just getting started. We'll be passing downtown Sacramento within fifteen minutes." I gave her a quick glance as she reached for the travel mug that sat in the cup holder. "Are you hungry?"

She moaned. "Not for at least another four hours." Rustling came from her side of the Jeep. "You must be a morning person."

"I'd say I'm a practical person, just like you. It just makes sense to drive."

"Depends on what kind of gas mileage you get with this thing."

"Better than a jet, I can tell you that."

She was silent for so long, I assumed she'd gone back to sleep.

"Can I ask you something?" Even though her voice was quiet, it cut through the dark.

"Sure."

She shifted her position. "When we met with Jerry last Saturday, he said something about everything you do for the outreach. What goes on there?"

"The Urban Outreach. It's exactly what it's called. A place people can go when they need help."

"What kind of help?"

I kept my gaze on the city lights up ahead. "Whatever you can think of. A lot of people who come in are homeless and need a place to live. We help them find Section 8 housing. Others need legal aid or a job."

"What do you do for them?"

"Whatever I can. Usually, I prepare them for a job interview or teach them how to keep a budget."

"How do you find time to do that with a full-time accounting business?"

I shrugged. "When God calls us to do something for Him, He stretches our time."

"How'd you end up volunteering there?"

"My grandfather. He had a real servant's heart and volunteered there for years. When I moved into his house, I took his spot."

"It sounds like all roads lead to your Grandpa."

"Funny." I smiled at her. "I thought all roads lead to Jesus."

She sighed. "I'm starting to sense that about you. We've spent so much time with Jake and Tess, I feel like I'm just beginning to know you. Maybe we should start over."

That was unexpected. "What do you mean?"

"Let's pretend we just met. You don't know anything about me, and I don't know anything about you."

I chuckled. "Really? What kind of woman jumps into the Jeep of a man she doesn't know?"

"A desperate one," she said. Then a heartbeat or two later, "But seriously, if we're going to be stuck in the car for eleven hours, what better way to spend the time than getting to know each other?"

Should I have been suspicious of her motives? "Full disclosure?"

"Yes. I'll ask the first question."

I glanced her way. "You already did."

"That was before we made the deal."

Arguing with her would've been pointless. Max didn't stand a chance when she wanted to debate an issue. "Fine. Shoot."

She folded her legs and cradled her tea between her hands. "What happened between you and Gillian?"

It took a moment to process her question. "Wow. You jump right into the deep end, don't you?"

Julia

As Marty and I bantered back and forth, my misgivings from last night about making this trip dwindled away like the receding waves of a tide. We were encased in the quiet darkness of the pre-dawn morning, and it made me bolder than I otherwise would have been.

Gillian. Just the name made me think tall, blond, and beautiful. Everything I wasn't. But a classy name did not a person make. And feeling insecure about a woman who was clearly out of the picture was a waste of time and energy. Still, knowing where Gillian went wrong might give me a clearer indication of the kind of man Marty was. This was important before we got too serious.

"So?" I urged him.

"Just so you know, the door swings both ways."

I could just make out his features in the glow of the dash lights. "What's that supposed to mean?"

"What's good for the goose is good for the gander."

Great. I was riding shotgun with the king of aphorisms. "Are you deflecting?"

"No. I'm just warning you. Two can play—"

"Enough already." I held up my hands. "Answer the question."

He blew out a breath. "What was it again?"

He was more aggravating than a five-year-old. "Gillian. You. What happened?"

He checked the rearview mirror before changing lanes to pass a semi. "While we were engaged, she was keeping her options open."

That was about as clear as mud. "You mean she wasn't sure she wanted to get married?"

"Let's just say she was auditioning other contenders. I was unaware she was the diva in an off-key bachelorette TV show."

His words marinated for a moment in my foggy, early-morning brain before the truth formed. "You mean she cheated on you." That wasn't unusual. Why the big secret?

"You make it sound so pedestrian."

"Cliché is more like it."

"Either way, it left me a little gun-shy when it comes to women. I was naive to think she was who she portrayed herself to be. Here I was, saving myself for marriage while she was playing the field."

"Saving yourself for marriage?" Shocker. "Are you saying you're a virgin?"

"Not exactly."

"Not exactly?"

"Could you please stop repeating everything I say?" He sounded more embarrassed than irritated.

"I'm sorry. I didn't mean to embarrass you."

He grimaced. "I have to admit, it's a little awkward to talk about. The truth is, when I matured in my faith, I recommitted my life to Christ, and that included being celibate until marriage. That was about five years ago."

"I'm guessing Gillian didn't hold to your views?"

"What she said and what she did were two different things."

I snorted. "Gillian doesn't sound any better than Stephen." Saving himself for marriage? How many men could say that?

"Speaking of..."

I waved a dismissive hand. "You already know all the dirt on him. I'm sure you can come up with something better."

"Okay, what's the deal with your parents?"

I would have assumed the question came from left field if I didn't recognize God's hand when I saw it. First Max, then Marty. *I hear you, Lord, loud and clear.* "You picked up on that, huh?"

"It's kind of hard to miss."

What's good for the goose. "I basically grew up in the O'Shay home. Tess and I have been friends since elementary school, and Sean's been a huge influence on my life."

"What does that have to do with your parents?"

"I'm setting the stage. You know, giving you the backstory. For whatever reason, they had an issue with Sean."

"Maybe your parents were jealous of your relationship with him."

I'd never thought of it in those terms. "Maybe. They aren't Christians, so when I started going to church, I got a lot of push back from them." Which made sense if they were jealous. Why had I not seen it before?

My explanation played catch-up with this new revelation. The jumbled pieces of my parental puzzle fell into place, and it was like God was revealing a truth I'd not seen before. "I suppose they felt some relief when I married Stephen, since he wasn't a Christian. And when we split, they blamed my faith." I replayed their accusations in my mind. "Funny. All this time, I thought my parents were rejecting me when I think maybe they felt I was rejecting them."

"You're just now realizing this?"

"Yes." I stared at Marty's profile, now clear in the rising sun. "As Tess pointed out the other day, this has certainly been an eye-opening few weeks."

"How so?" Marty's eyes flickered on me for a brief moment.

"It's just amazing how a little change in perspective clears things up. Suffice it to say, I have some fences to mend. You're pretty good at this."

"What? Talking?"

"It's more than that. You're intuitive. I think you have some great insights."

He looked at me, eyebrows arched. "You're sleep deprived."

"True." I reached for my tea. "My turn."

"Hit me."

I hesitated a beat or two. One question had been tapping at my brain ever since Marty hinted at feelings for me. Did I really want to hear his answer? Could I move forward with him otherwise? "Before Tess and Jake got together, did you have a thing for her?"

He gave me a crooked grin. "That's an easy one. No."

I squinted at him. "Yeah, right. You're going to tell me you weren't attracted to her?"

"That's not what you asked. I'd be lying if I said I hadn't been attracted to her."

"If you didn't have a thing for her, why'd you keep asking her out?"

"Because it got under Jake's skin. The first time I met Tess was when I was helping Jake move his things into her guest house. The tension between the two of them was thick as taffy. Even if I'd been deaf, dumb, and blind, I would've felt the connection between them."

"I don't get it."

"Jake just needed a little push to step up to the plate. I was the nudge."

"But what if she'd agreed to go out with you?"

He laughed. "There was no way she'd have gone out with me, and I knew it. She only had eyes for Jake. The two of them were almost nauseating."

The tension in my shoulders eased. "I've thought the exact same thing." I wouldn't mind it so much if someone said the same thing about Marty and me someday.

"Besides, I love home-cooked meals, and the word on the street is Tess can't cook."

I grinned. "Did Jake tell you that?"

"Jake, Katie, Sean." He barked out a laugh. "You know what they say about a man's stomach."

"Yeah, but I'm not buying it." Even so, his innuendo warmed my insides like *créme brûlée*.

Chapter 13

Julia

With only a few fuel and bathroom breaks, we arrived in Glendale by four. Driving wasn't nearly as bad as I'd anticipated. It was clear Marty had the whole commute thing down —he'd brought plenty of snacks and a case of bottled water. Since the entire trip was for my benefit, I should have been the one to do that. Instead, I'd acted more like a rebellious child dependent on his charity than a grown woman. Shame on me.

The weather cooperated, and although it was clear and below freezing when we'd left Placerville, Glendale was a balmy mid-60's. Throughout the long drive, I could have almost forgotten the reason behind it. But once we'd seen the city sign, my heart beat like a bass drum, and it became hard to breathe. What was my fear based on? That I might find Stephen or that I might not?

Marty pulled the Jeep up to a gas pump, and I turned to him. "We're really doing this."

He turned off the ignition. "Having second thoughts?"

"No." I sucked air into my lungs. *Relax.*

He took my hand. "If you don't want to do this, say the word. We can grab dinner and head back."

I narrowed my eyes. "You'd do that?"

"If that's what you want. We can stop in San Diego, stay at my parents' place tonight, and hit the road in the morning. I'm here to support you either way." His face was relaxed. No lines of frustration etched around his mouth. No censure in his gaze.

How was it possible he could be so amenable?

"Well, Jules. What's it going to be?"

"We don't even know if he's still at that motel."

"Jerry downloaded the app he used onto my phone. He may not be there, but his phone is. Of course, we don't know what room he's in. You know what to do, right?"

"Yes. I'll go up to the front desk and tell them that I'm supposed to meet my husband but don't remember what room he's in. I'll show the desk clerk my driver's license if I need to for verification."

"And you have Stephen's photo if you need it to identify him?"

"Yes." I was going to be sick. "I don't think I'm cut out for detective work."

"In for a penny." He shrugged.

I scowled. "What is it with you and the sayings?"

"Just one of the many quirks Gramps handed down to me."

"No disrespect to your grandfather, but it's a little annoying."

"Enough with the stalling. Why don't you let me go with you?"

I crossed my arms over my roiling stomach and pressed my back into the passenger seat. "I appreciate it, Marty, but Stephen's more apt to talk to me if I'm alone."

"I'd feel better if you weren't by yourself, Jules."

"I'll be fine. The worst that can happen is Stephen's angry

at me for showing up. It wouldn't be the first time I've upset him."

As Marty drove the few blocks to the motel, I tried to center my thoughts. I'd thought about what I would say to him but had no idea how he'd respond. I didn't want to make matters worse and coming across as a hysterical female would only put Stephen on the defensive. So, how should I approach him?

I glanced at Marty who was maneuvering through heavy traffic. "Working with the Urban Outreach, you've dealt with situations like this before, right?"

A grin flirted around the corners of his mouth. "Not really. Clients come to me. I don't have to track them down."

I waved my hands as if to erase my words. "I mean, if you were Stephen, what tactic would work best?"

He frowned. "You know better than anyone how to reach him. I can't imagine he won't be moved by the effort you took to find him."

"I guess."

He pulled up to a red light, stopped, and turned to look at me. "Before you know what to say to him, you need to know what you hope to accomplish. You also need to know what kind of trouble he's in."

I nodded.

"Do you think he's a threat? Because if you do, there's no way I can just sit outside while you go in."

"Stephen wouldn't hurt me." That much I knew.

The flow of traffic moved again, and within five minutes we pulled into the parking lot of the rundown motel. There was an empty dirt lot next door and a few trees interspersed along the street.

Marty put the Jeep in park. "Once you have the room number, I'll move the car so I can be close by in case you need me."

My legs were stiff as steel rods as I made my way into the

hotel. *If you don't want me to do this, Lord, now's the time to intervene.*
Nothing resembling divine intervention halted my progress to
the front desk where a young woman stood, her focus on a
computer screen.

I cleared my throat to get her attention. "Hi, I'm—"

"Just one sec, ma'am." Her fingers flew over the keyboard,
then she clicked the mouse and looked up. "You need a
room?"

"No. Um, actually, I'm meeting my husband here, and I
can't remember the room number."

"What's his name?"

"Stephen Metcalf." I slid his photo onto the desk.

She glared at the photo and frowned. "You have ID?"

My hands were shaking so hard, it took a couple tries to
unlatch my purse. I pulled out my wallet and flipped it open so
she could see my driver's license.

"He's in eighteen. It's across the lot at the end."

"Thank you."

Once outside, I walked to Marty's car and stepped up to
his window. "Room 18." I pointed to the end.

He arched his brows. "You sure you want to do this
alone?"

"You'll be right outside."

A window, covered with thick draperies, was next to the
motel room door. When I stepped up to Stephen's room, the
sound of my heartbeat drowned out all else. The draperies
moved, but the glare on the glass prevented me from getting a
clear view.

The door swung open and Stephen stood there. "Julia.
What are you doing here?"

This was not the man I had married—or even the one who'd
left me. This Stephen was living like a mole, hunkered down

in a cave-like room. The blinds were closed, cloaking the room in shadows and stale air. Take out boxes littered the dresser and nightstands. Clothes were strewn across the bed and chairs. He was dressed in a grubby t-shirt and jeans. Body odor emanated from him, and he was in desperate need of a shave.

I stepped back and resisted the urge to cover my nose. "A better question is what are *you* doing here?"

His gaze darted from the door and back at me. "Are you alone?"

"No. A friend brought me."

"Tess?"

"It doesn't matter who." I folded my arms. There were bags under his eyes, and he looked like he'd lost weight. I couldn't decide whether to smack him or hug him. "What kind of trouble have you gotten yourself into?"

He dropped onto the edge of the bed, head low. "How'd you find me?"

I scooped up the clothes piled onto the chair and dumped them on the floor before sitting. "It wasn't all that hard, actually. It's not like you went to any great lengths to hide. You registered here under your own name."

"What was I supposed to do? They require ID. Besides, you and my mom are the only two who know where I went. I ditched my cell phone, which is why I texted you with a new number."

I grimaced. "I don't think I'd have been able to find you if you hadn't contacted me. How long did you have this planned, anyway? I went to your apartment the day after we talked, and it was like you were never there."

"I had to be out before the first of the month. I stayed with a friend the last two weeks."

"You could have told me that when we talked last. Instead, you let me believe you were still in the planning stage of moving."

"And you would've wanted to know why."

I rubbed my forehead. "Well, yeah. We might be divorced, Stephen, but you're still Max's father."

He looked at me and sighed. "I'm not cut out for this, Jules."

"Who is? So, what happened?"

He stood slowly, like he'd aged ten years, and crossed to the window. With the tuck of a finger, he moved the curtain a mere three inches and peered outside. "I took out a bad loan, and then I tried to cover it by betting on a sure thing."

I gritted my teeth to bite back a reprimand. "There's no such animal."

"Yeah." He turned to me. "I don't know what to do." His resemblance to a distraught Max threw me off, but it reminded me why I was here.

"I must have tried to call a hundred times."

He nodded. "I didn't want to talk to anyone."

"And you couldn't have been bothered to answer a text either?" It wouldn't get me anywhere if I went on attack. I took a deep breath and continued. "This doesn't just affect you, Stephen."

His head bobbed as if he agreed with me. "I know, Jules. You depend on child support and—"

"That's the least of it, Stephen. Am I right to assume this guy, Glen, is who you're running from?"

"Yeah."

"You got the message that he came by the restaurant looking for you?"

"Yeah. Sorry about that."

"And when he didn't get what he wanted, he broke into my house."

When he just looked at me, heat crawled up my neck, and I gritted my teeth. "I texted you, Stephen. I told you that your actions put Max and me in danger, and you didn't even bother to respond. What kind of a father puts his son in danger?" My voice cracked as a sob rose to the surface. "You might not care a fig about me, but what about Max?" Tears burned at the back of my eyes, and I blinked them away.

Stephen stared at me like I was speaking in tongues. "I didn't know."

"I'm not buying that." I swiped at the tears and stood. The need to pace thrummed through me, but the room was too small. "You're going to tell me you didn't get my texts?"

"I didn't look at them." He jammed his hands into the front pockets of his jeans. "I'm sorry."

I curled my fingers into the palms of my hands and took a couple of deep breaths. Rehashing what was already done wouldn't be productive.

"Jules." He reached a hand toward me, and I backed away. "Believe me, I'm really sorry. If I had any idea…"

"What?" I looked him in the eye. "What would you have done, Stephen?"

"What d'you want me to do?" He dropped onto the edge of the cluttered desk, and a Chinese takeout box tumbled to the floor.

I shook my head. "I don't know. I guess I want you to make it right. If someone's after you, sitting in this hotel room isn't going to fix the problem. You need to go to the police."

His eyes widened. "And tell them what? I'm guilty here, too. Everything's so black and white with you. It's not that simple."

I rubbed my forehead. "Yes, Stephen, it is that simple. You make it complicated."

"So, I turn myself in? I could go to jail. There's got to be a better solution."

"You can't hide out here forever." I waved an arm to encompass the room. He was already in a prison of his own making. "Talk to an attorney."

He snorted. "Attorneys cost money. I'm homeless, jobless, and broke."

"I realize that, Stephen, but I'm sure there are options available out there. What happened to your job?"

Eyes down, he shrugged. "My references didn't pan out."

That was what happened when you walked out on a perfectly good job without notice. But pointing it out would be like pouring acid on the wound. Even as angry as I was with him, I didn't have the heart.

"What about your mom?"

The sag of his shoulders dropped by a couple inches as if the load got heavier. "I suppose she'd let me stay with her, but she doesn't have money for a lawyer either."

Hadn't Marty said the Urban Outreach helped with legal aid? Would Stephen qualify? Even if he does, would Marty be willing to help? Of course, he would. Hadn't he said he'd help any way he could? "I may have a solution to your attorney issue."

Chapter 14

Marty

Downtown Glendale was lit up with more Christmas decorations than I'd ever seen in one place. Every tree, every building, every everything exploded with lights. Santa's elves hadn't stuck with the traditional red and green either. They'd gone over the top with blue, purple, and white, too.

I wasn't sure what I expected once Julia found Stephen. I hadn't really thought that far in advance. But of course, he would be in dire straits; that's why he disappeared in the first place. My experience at the Urban Outreach taught me to see people as a whole, and not the sum of their mistakes. It was a little harder to do in this situation since it was personal. But then, I hadn't expected him to be sitting across a dinner table from me.

The Mexican restaurant was busy. Probably not unusual for a Thursday night, but the noise level grated. There were red pepper lights strung around the windows—whether they were part of the normal decor or a concession to Christmas, I didn't know. After the long trip and little sleep, it was all I could do to be coherent.

Stephen plucked a tortilla chip from the basket in the middle of the table then leaned toward me. "Jules says you can help me out."

"Maybe." Julia's response was like a gunshot—quick and loud. She touched my arm as if to maintain a united front. "I told you, Stephen, I couldn't make any promises."

I slumped in my chair, the wooden back biting into my shoulder blades. While waiting in the Jeep for Stephen to join us, Julia and I had talked briefly about his situation. "What are you hoping I can do for you?"

He popped the chip into his mouth then reached for his beer. "Well,"—he took a pull and swallowed—"legal aid for starters." He nodded at Julia. "She said you work with a group that helps out people in my situation."

"That's true. I work with the marginalized and those who have fallen on hard times. We have a great team."

His head bounced like a bobble head. "Well, I gotta say, I've fallen on pretty hard times."

"So it would seem." From what Julia told me, it sounded like Stephen needed more than legal help, but we would need to take it one step at a time.

I rested my elbows on the table. "My advice is to start by going to the police. From what I understand, you could be in physical danger, and—"

"I could go to jail." His gaze flickered between Julia and me.

"*And*"—I continued as if he hadn't spoken—"you should turn in that guy Glen."

He wrapped a hand around the beer bottle and shook his head. "I can't do that."

"If we get you an attorney, they'll give you the same advice. This guy accosted Julia at work, trailed her around town, broke into her house and trashed it. Both she and Max are in danger now. If you aren't willing to take the first step, I don't know how to help."

"Now hold on a minute." He pushed his hands through his hair. "Just hear me out, will you? I'm sorry that my problems came down on them, but isn't there another way to handle this?"

Julia leaned forward. "Think about it, Stephen. What choice do you have?"

Stephen's mouth drew into a tight line. After a few moments, he sighed. "Fine. What do we do first?"

"Order dinner," I said. "We'll all think better with a little food in our systems."

Julia placed her hand on mine. "I'm going to run to the ladies' room. If the waiter comes before I return, could you order me a taco salad with chicken?"

"Sure thing." I looked at Stephen. "What are you hungry for?"

Stephen rallied enough to reach for his menu. While still glancing at it, he said, "What's with you two, anyway? Are you dating?"

If I had a future with Julia, there was a good chance Stephen would be part of it. Still, I wasn't comfortable sharing personal information with him yet. As far as I was concerned, he was a stranger, and I needed to stay in counseling mode. "That's something you should ask Julia." I took a gulp of iced tea.

Watching me from under hooded eyes, he snatched a chip from the bowl and broke it in half. "You just don't seem like her type is all."

"Really? And what type is that?"

He shrugged. "She's hung up on religion, you know."

"Is that so?"

He nodded. "It's what broke us up. Always harping on me about church. And then, of course, there's Max."

"Yeah?"

"I mean, he's a great kid and all, but her world revolves around him."

I took a chip from the bowl and popped it into my mouth, giving me time to formulate a response. "How much time have you spent with Max?"

Frowning, he glanced at me. "What d'you mean?"

"You share custody, right? Are you with him every weekend, every other weekend, once a month?"

He picked up his beer and sat back. "I know what you're getting at."

I lifted my hands, palms up. "I'm just making conversation here."

"You don't think I spend enough time with Max."

"It's not what I think that matters, Stephen. If you don't see Max that often—and I'm not saying you don't—then Julia may feel a need to compensate."

He kept his gaze on the bottle. "Did Julia tell you I didn't see my own dad much growing up?"

"No." I took a chip and broke it in two. "That must've been hard."

He nodded.

"I grew up going to church, so I guess you'd say I'm hung up on religion, too. The truth of it, though, has nothing to do with religion and everything to do with relationship."

"What's the difference?"

"Religion is about the rules and laws we read about in the Old Testament. Relationship is what we have with God because Jesus paid the price for our inability to follow the rules." It might have been a simplistic explanation, but I hoped it made sense.

I leaned my elbows on the table. "When I was a kid, there was a Scripture verse that scared me. It was in Numbers, which is a book in the Old Testament, and spoke about the sins of the father being passed down on the children to the third and fourth generations."

"Are you saying God'll punish Max for the things I do

wrong?" He shook his head. "And Julia wonders why I don't buy into the whole church thing. How is that fair?"

I held up a hand. "That's not what I'm saying. That's the problem with taking Scripture out of context. I would love the opportunity to delve further into this later, but for now, the point I'm so poorly trying to make is that you have suffered because of your dad's neglect. God didn't punish you; it was the consequence of your father's issues. Maybe he suffered because of his father's shortcomings as well."

He nodded. "That kind of makes sense."

"You can change that, Stephen. I hope you don't make the same mistake with Max that your dad did with you. Julia is an amazing, beautiful woman, and it's partly due to her relationship with Jesus. You might not want to disregard the chance at a relationship with God. It could literally change your life."

His eyes flickered behind me, and I turned to see Julia standing there, eyes shiny with tears.

Julia

When we were done and Marty had paid the bill, we stood outside the restaurant and watched Stephen melt into the dark. He'd agreed to call Margaret with the hope she'd let him stay with her while he dealt with his legal issues. He said he would make a full confession to the Placerville police of all that had transpired between him and Glen. Then on Monday, Marty would meet him at the Urban Outreach to set him up with legal aid and anything else he might need.

"Baby, It's Cold Outside" accompanied the Christmas decor through invisible speakers, and the entire Old Towne was dazzling. Still, I wanted to be back in Placerville and get back to some kind of normalcy. I wanted to be snuggled on my couch watching *How the Grinch Stole Christmas* with Max while we snacked on cinnamon and sugar popcorn as had become our Christmas tradition.

"There has to be at least a million lights strung out here." Marty's eyes were focused on the brilliant Christmas display. "Do you want to walk a while or go back to the motel?" He glanced at his watch. "If we're going to take off at three, we should probably turn in soon."

I needed a chance to decompress and feel Marty out about the meeting with Stephen. Then again, we'd have an eleven-hour drive to do that. Still, I wasn't quite ready to face a sterile motel room. "Let's walk for a few minutes."

"Okay." We strolled in silence for a couple blocks, his eyes glittering with the reflection of the twinkle lights before he put an arm around my shoulder. "How do you think things went tonight?"

The weight of his arm was comforting, and I allowed myself the luxury of sinking into his warmth while I contemplated the question. I couldn't imagine being in Stephen's position, but he seemed determined to get his life back on track. "I think you were pretty great with him. When I came back from the bathroom, his whole attitude had shifted." We stepped around a group milling in front of a restaurant.

"We don't know the extent of his involvement, but I think he has a pretty good chance of avoiding jail time. Maybe getting a break will be the impetus he needs to make some changes."

"All the time we were married, I tried to talk to him about a relationship with God. Nothing sunk in. Then you talk to him for five minutes, and he hangs on your every word."

Marty chuckled. "I doubt that. If he listened to me at all it was because of God's timing. You planted the seeds, I did a little watering, and now it's up to the Holy Spirit to do the heavy lifting. Sometimes we have to be at rock bottom before anything sinks in."

"I was a fool to marry him, knowing he wasn't a Christian.

I let my ego get the better of me. I've accused Stephen of being foolish, but I was no better."

"You're being a little hard on yourself, don't you think? Love makes us do crazy things."

"I think it was more lust and insecurity," I said. "I couldn't believe Stephen was attracted to me in the first place, and when he asked me to marry him…let's just say I should have been prayerful about it."

Marty's arm tightened around my shoulder as he dropped a kiss on my temple. Warmth thrummed through my body. "I don't think God lets our mistakes derail His plans for us. It might be that your relationship with Stephen was necessary for him to surrender his life to Christ. It's not always about us."

Wasn't that the truth.

"I'm beginning to sense a pattern here," Marty said.

"What's that?"

"A few weeks back, I made the offhand comment that you're beautiful, and you seemed uncomfortable. I didn't know if it was the compliment or the fact that I was the one giving it to you that caused it. Just now, you said you were insecure, and you couldn't believe Stephen found you attractive."

Heat climbed up my neck and settled in my cheeks. He'd told Stephen I was beautiful and amazing. When was the last time I'd heard those words in reference to myself? "I admit there have been bouts of insecurity. Who wouldn't want to look like a supermodel?"

"'The Lord does not look at the things man looks at. Man looks at the outward appearance, but the Lord looks at the heart.'" He fingered a strand of hair off my cheek. "I know that verse was meant for the anointing of King David in the Old Testament, but I think it applies here. When I told Stephen you're beautiful and amazing, I meant it. I'm attracted to you, Julia. I love your smile and the shape of your eyes. I love your tenderness with Max and your quick wit.

Whether you lose a few pounds or gain a few pounds, it doesn't change who you are."

A knot of emotion filled my throat, and I dropped my eyes to hide the shame I knew lurked there. Had I not been guilty of judging by outward appearances, I would have never been attracted to Stephen. And at the same time, I judged Marty unworthy because I'd not taken the time to get to know him.

"Hey, what's with the tears?" He hooked a finger under my chin and lifted it then thumbed away a tear I hadn't even known was there.

"I'm as much of a fool as Stephen," I whispered.

"It's okay if you don't feel the same about me."

I shook my head. "It's not that." A sob cut off my voice, and I had to take a moment to gain control of my emotions. "I've been just as guilty of focusing on outward appearances and look where it got me. Married to a man with the heart of a fool and dismissing a man with the heart of gold."

He pulled me in for a hug, his chin resting on my head. His heart beat against my ear along with the rumble of his voice. "You're in good company, Jules. I was about five minutes away from marrying Gillian which would have been the biggest mistake of my life. At least you got Max out of the deal. Not a bad trade-off."

Leave it to Marty to point out the silver lining.

Chapter 15

Julia

White icicle-lights outlined my childhood home, glimmering in the early evening dusk. A Christmas tree, also lit up with white lights, filled the front window. Neighboring houses were similarly decorated as if the owners were following association guidelines. It was both beautiful and disturbing—a little too "Stepford Wives" for my taste.

As I climbed out of the car, I glanced up at the window above the garage where my bedroom had been. No light shone through it, and I imagined it was as closed off as my relationship with my parents. Out of sight, out of mind? Cynicism would get me nowhere but frustrated. I shook it off as I climbed the steps to the front door where a fake snow-encrusted swag of pine hung with a *"Merry Christmas"* banner plastered across it. Red berries, pinecones and a real ice skate was attached to it. No one did Christmas quite like Mom.

I wanted this conversation to go well—prayed for it. Armed with wise counsel from Tess and Marty, a few pieces of Scripture, and a desire to understand my parents' perspective, I waited. My palms were clammy, and my heart beat like the *rat tat tat* of "The Little Drummer Boy." At least it would be one-on-one this time since Dad was out of town on business. Mom hadn't asked why I wanted to stop by, and I hadn't given any hints.

The door swung open, and I was faced with Mom's hesitant smile. That was a positive sign, wasn't it? Her salon-perfect dark hair brushed her slender shoulders. The jeans and a red sweater she wore looked better on her than they would a woman half her age. Wish I'd gotten those genes—no pun intended. She glanced past me then back again.

"He's at a friend's," I explained before she could ask about Max.

Her smile wavered then reset as she opened the door wider. "Come in out of the cold, Julia." She was making an effort.

Shrugging out of my coat, I stepped into the tiled foyer. A smaller Christmas tree was nestled into the corner by the stairs. It looked like something that could grace the front cover of *Home & Garden* magazine with its burgundy and silver color-coordinated ornaments. I didn't have to take another step to know that every room would be likewise endowed. It's how Mom rolled. A quick calculation in my head reminded me I only had two weeks before decorating for the holidays would be moot.

"The house looks nice, Mom." I gave her an awkward hug, my purse and coat getting hung up in the mix.

"Thanks." She led the way into the kitchen. "Can I get you something? A glass of wine, maybe?"

"Wine would put me to sleep before I could get Max's dinner on the table. Do you have any tea?"

"Sure." She filled a teal-blue kettle and put it on the stove.

Ten minutes later, mugs in hand, we retreated to the family room. Greenery and candles nestled on the fireplace mantle above the four stockings that hung in a perfect row. Mom sat in a tapestry-upholstered recliner, and I settled on the couch. The furniture was new, and I took a brief moment to admire Mom's taste. Was there anything she didn't do well?

"It's been too long." Mom took a tentative sip from her cup.

I retrieved a coaster from a small drawer in the coffee table—at least that was familiar—and set my tea down. "Life has been a little crazy lately." To say the least.

"How's Max doing?" She slipped off her shoes and tucked her legs beneath her.

"He's good." Fingers intertwined, I rested them on my lap. How do I even start this discussion? I didn't want to put her on the defensive, but I also didn't want to crumble under the pressure of needing to please. "Look, Mom." I cleared my throat. "The reason I didn't bring Max with me is because I want to talk to you about something, and I didn't want him to distract us."

"Oh?" Head tilted slightly, and she frowned. "What's going on? Do you need money?"

"No," I said, sharper than intended. I unclenched my fingers and rubbed my temple where a drum solo was starting to play. "It's not about money."

Concern clouded her eyes. "You're not sick, are you?" Her whole body stiffened as if she was preparing for a blow.

I shook my head. "No, Mom. It's nothing like that." Sudden tears burned at the back of my eyes. "It's *us*."

"Us?" Her eyebrows disappeared behind wispy bangs. "You and me, us?"

Swallowing back the ridiculous tears, I nodded. "I want us to get along, you know?"

"What are you talking about? We get along." She waved a dismissive hand and reached for her tea.

Marty's words of advice came back to me. *Say what you mean and mean what you say.* I slid down to the end of the couch, close enough to touch her. "You're right, Mom. We get along. We're polite and cordial whenever we see each other, but it's not enough. I feel as if there's a wall between us and has been since I was a kid."

She looked away from me and shrugged. Bingo.

"You feel it too, don't you?" I touched her knee. What I wanted to do was climb up into her lap like I did when I was Max's age and ask her to make it all better. It was around the time I began hanging out at Tess's house that I stopped leaning on her for support.

"I suppose."

"Was it something I did?" I pressed my hand to my heart. "I know you were disappointed when Stephen and I got divorced, but—"

"It wasn't that." She crossed her arms. A defensive move if I ever saw one.

"It's because I became a Christian, isn't it?" The words hung in the air as if not finding a safe place to land. "Or was it because of the influence Tess's family had on me?"

"Does it matter?" Her tone was the same weary shade I saw in her eyes.

"I think it does." I reached across the expanse and covered her hand with mine. "I never intended to hurt you and Dad."

Tears filled her eyes as she looked at me. "You're going to think it's ridiculous. It's just…"

I felt as if we were on the brink of the first honest conversation we'd had in years. "What?" I squeezed her hand. "Tell me."

She hooked her hair behind her ear—a move I had inherited from her. "They had everything. A wonderful marriage, two beautiful daughters, a successful business." Her gaze caught mine. "We only had you. It seemed you were happiest when you were with them."

I swiped at the tears that slipped down my cheeks. A heaviness filled my chest at the hurt in her voice. "I'm sorry." What else could I say? She was right. "I thought maybe you were upset because I became a Christian."

She shrugged. "I suppose we were, in a way. I mean, that was part of their whole appeal, wasn't it?"

"Only because they understood how much I loved Jesus. With you, it seemed like a character flaw."

"I didn't see it as a flaw, Julia."

"But later, when Stephen and I split up, you said it was because I was a Christian, as if that was a bad thing."

She hesitated a moment. "From my limited perspective, it seemed as if you put your religion above your marriage. I just thought if you had put Stephen first, he might not have cheated on you."

I shook my head. "It wouldn't have mattered, Mom. Stephen isn't who you think he is."

"Then why'd you marry him?"

Good question. Hadn't Marty asked the same thing? "I didn't see it." I grimaced. "He was gorgeous, and I let it blind me to his true character. Which, by the way, goes way beyond infidelity."

"You weren't blind, sweetheart. You were human."

"Maybe, but God's been showing me how wrong my snap judgments have been."

She frowned. "What do you mean *God's* been showing you? He doesn't actually talk to you, does He?"

Did I detect a hint of curiosity in her tone?

By the time I got Max fed, listened to him read two chapters of *Addison Cooke*, and helped him with his math homework, I was exhausted but joyful. Mom and I had taken two giant steps toward a closer relationship. Since Dad wasn't scheduled to return from his trip until Wednesday, she was going to meet Max and me for dinner at the restaurant tomorrow night. Her curiosity about my *relationship* with Jesus—not *religion*, I pointed out to her—was piqued. What better place to rebuild a faulty foundation than with Jesus?

"So, it went well?" Tess asked over the phone.

I held the cell between my chin and shoulder in order to fold the pile of laundry I'd dumped onto one end of the couch. "Better than well. It was the first real conversation we've had in years. There were no snide comments or rude innuendoes. And Mom behaved, too."

Tess chuckled. "That's amazing, Jules. There sure has been a lot of relationship shifting for you lately."

"Tell me about it. I was—"

The doorbell cut off the rest of my sentence. It was after nine. Who'd show up that late? "There's someone here." I stared at the door as if the visitor would somehow be revealed through two inches of solid wood.

"At this time of night?" I could hear her suck in a breath. "What if it's the creep who broke in?"

Glen? "I doubt it."

"Make sure you ask who it is before you open the door," Tess said.

"Yes, *Mom*." I inched toward the door and flipped on the porch light. I had to wrestle with the bough of the Christmas tree to peer through the slats of the blinds covering the front window. Great. "It's Stephen." His posture was slumped, but his hair and clothes were clean and tidy. He definitely looked better than he did when I confronted him at the motel on Thursday night.

"You're not going to let him in, are you?" Tess sounded as indignant as I felt.

"I gotta go."

"Call me when he leaves."

I leaned against the door, the phone to my chest. "What do you want, Stephen?"

"Can we talk?" His response through the door was muffled.

"It's late, and I'm too tired. Can it wait until tomorrow?"

"Five minutes, Jules."

I chewed at my bottom lip. I really, really didn't want to do this now.

"Please, Jules. I just want to let you know how things went today."

With an exaggerated sigh, I opened the door. "Okay. Five minutes."

He shuffled in and looked around as if he expected to see Max. First Mom, now Stephen. A woman could get an inferiority complex.

"He's in bed. It's after nine, you know."

He combed a hand through his curls and plopped onto the couch, toppling the folded and stacked laundry. "Oh, yeah. I guess I lost track of the time. Nice tree. You have anything to drink?"

"I don't want to be rude, Stephen, but you won't be here long enough to drink anything, unless it's water. I'd be happy to get you a glass." I sandwiched piles of clothes between my hands and moved them, one by one, from the couch to the basket. Leave it to Stephen to be here less than thirty seconds and create more work for me.

"You're in a mood."

"Sorry." I slid the basket against the wall. "It's been a long day." I perched on the edge of my recliner—not nearly as classy as Mom's—and crossed my arms. "Now you have four minutes."

He raised his hands as if staving off my attitude. "Fine. Sheesh. Thought you'd like to know I met with someone from legal aid today."

"So, I take it you went to the police and turned Glen in?"

"Yes." He bit the word off then slumped back on the couch. "Your boyfriend didn't give me any choice, did he?"

The automatic response, "He's not my boyfriend" was on the tip of my tongue, but I swallowed it down. If he wasn't my boyfriend, then what was he? "Of course you had a choice. But you asked for his advice, and he gave it to you. How'd it go with the attorney?"

His features relaxed. "He thinks I'll get off with some community service as long as I give them everything I know about Glen's operation, and I'm willing to testify." He crossed his arms. "They'll probably have more questions for you too, since he broke in."

"And you're staying with your mom?"

A muscle jumped in his jaw, but he nodded. That must be hard. I certainly wouldn't want to live with my mom again, even with our improved connection.

"What are your plans? Are you going to try and get back on with PG&E?"

He shrugged. "You think I should?"

"It can't hurt to try. How did you leave it with them? Did you give notice?"

"Not exactly."

I blew out a breath. "Then your guess is as good as mine. Maybe you should talk to this attorney you met with at the center. There may be something he can do for you."

"I never thought of that."

"The first thing you should figure out is if you want to stay here. Was leaving only motivated by your problems with Glen, or do you really find it hard to afford it here?"

"I don't know what difference it makes if I'm here or somewhere else."

I pinched the bridge of my nose and took a deep breath. How could I possibly reach him? "Look, Stephen, I know you didn't have much of a father figure in your life. But that doesn't mean you can't become the kind of father Max deserves—the kind of father you deserved growing up. Your dad was flawed, but there is One who isn't."

His mouth grew tight, and he slowly nodded. "You and

Marty are trying to tag team me, huh?" At least he knew where I was heading. That was something, wasn't it?

I shrugged. "You do you, Stephen. I just hope you realize in that equation somewhere, Max counts. He needs you."

"What for? He's got your boyfriend, doesn't he?"

"No one can take your place in Max's heart. You just need to decide how important that is to you."

He pushed off from the couch, and without another word, walked out the door.

Chapter 16

Marty

For the first time since Gram passed, the old house had life. Gramps might have been alive another few years, but he was never himself again. It had been a sad sight—the old man and the bachelor grandson knocking around the place. After he died, I couldn't seem to get up the gumption—one of Gramp's words—to make the place my own.

Then Julia happened. *Mi casa, es su casa.* She hadn't asked twice if I'd meant it. Max and I had cut down a tree while Julia worked the day before, and now Max and his friend Keith were in the family room throwing tinsel on it. The tantalizing smells coming from the kitchen, pine boughs on the mantle, and scented candles throughout the house turned it from ordinary to party-ready in a mere few hours.

I found a classical Christmas station on Pandora and filled the house with singers from Gram and Gramp's generation— Frank Sinatra, Burl Ives, Nat King Cole. A bittersweet knot formed in my throat as I wandered into the kitchen where Julia had every conceivable counter space covered with candied nuts, chocolate cake, butter cream, and things I couldn't even identify.

She stood at the stove manning pots of bubbling concoctions. Her hair was pulled up into a clip, perspiration glistening on her upper lip and forehead. She wore a bright red apron over her jeans—something Gram would have done. The quick smile she gave me melted into a frown. "Are you okay?"

I pilfered a warm cookie from a cooling rack, broke off a piece, and popped it into my mouth. Ginger. "Just trying to stay out of the line of fire."

"I'm sorry." She looked around the room and her frown deepened. "I made myself at home, didn't I?"

"I hope so. It's what I wanted you to do." I finished off the cookie. A hint of heaven.

"You look a little sad."

I leaned my backside against the counter, careful to not disturb the clutter, and tucked my hands into the front pockets of my jeans. "Not sad. A little nostalgic, maybe. The last time there was any kind of holiday celebration here was when my grandmother was still alive."

She swiped the back of her wrist across her forehead. "You miss them."

I shrugged. "It's amazing to me how quickly time passes. The older we get…"

"The faster it goes," she finished. Her coffee-colored eyes softened as they met mine. "Even though you offered, it was pushy of me to do all this." She opened her arms to encompass the room.

"I'm glad you did." I pulled a hand from my pocket and waved her over. "Come 'ere."

She crossed the room and stepped into my arms, her own wrapping around my waist as she nestled against me and sighed. Her body fit mine as if we were made for each other. No way I was going to say that out loud, though. Wouldn't

Jake have a field day with *that* comment? Still, I never wanted Julia to be in doubt about my feelings.

"My prayer, Jules, is that this will be your home someday. You're the best thing that's happened to me in a very long time."

"I feel the same way," she said against my chest. "I don't know why it took us so long."

"Timing," I said.

"Hey, Mom." Max's voice cut into the moment with the impact of a cymbal crash.

Julia stepped back just as he appeared. "Sadly, the kid's way off," she said before turning to him. "What happened to your inside voice?"

"We're done with the tree. Can we go outside and play?"

She glanced at her watch. "One hour. But stay near the house. No wandering down to the creek or going into the pear orchard. Got it?"

"Got it." He ran from the room yelling, "We can go outside now!"

Julia shook her head and grimaced. "You may want to rethink this relationship, Marty. We're a package deal."

I ran a knuckle down her cheek. "A very cute package. What do you need me to do?"

She chewed on her lower lip, eyes drifting into think mode. "I'm not sure. Tess should be here soon with the rest of the food."

"The *rest* of the food?" My gaze took in what appeared to be enough for a third-world country. "You mean there's more?"

"These are just the desserts."

"You mean Tess is bringing the main course?"

"Yes. Why?"

"She didn't cook it, did she?"

Julia's eyes cleared and she laughed. "What? And give

everyone food poisoning? Sean cooked. Tess is just the delivery person. Plus, she's great at washing dishes."

"Yeah? I'm pretty good with dishes, too."

She poked my stomach with a finger. "You're the one who put the boys on tree decorating duty. I think maybe you should inspect their work. Knowing Max, it's probably not up to my standards. And it's definitely not going to be up to my mom's standards." She rolled her eyes.

"Look, Jules." I slipped my hand into hers and cupped her cheek with the other. "I'm thrilled that you and your parents are back on even ground."

"Me too," she said.

"And I'm happy they wanted to be here tonight."

She nodded.

"But I'd hate to see you tie yourself into knots trying to be something other than who you are." I dropped her chin and wrapped my arm around her shoulders. "It's a slippery slope, babe. Your mom may be—what was it you called her? The decorating queen?—but I'd bet my IRA you cook circles around her. And you're pretty spectacular in the Mom category, too."

She pulled back to smile at me. "You're sweet."

I shook my head. "I'm not being sweet. I'm being honest. I love you exactly as you are."

She held my gaze. "Then you should know that I have no desire to be a decorating queen. I love that about my mom because it's how she expresses her creativity. I can hang a picture or two, and I'm capable of painting a wall. But that's as far as it goes. And since we're talking preferences, I prefer cooking to housework, although I'm not opposed to the idea of you with a vacuum."

She followed up her little speech with a smirk that let me know life would never be dull with this woman.

❄

Julia

I'd always heard that Easter was a season of new beginnings. After all, it was the celebration of the day Jesus rose from the dead. But for me, this Christmas would forever stand out as a time of rebirth. New relationships. Repaired relationships. Unexpected grace.

About an hour into the party, I perched on a riser halfway up the stairs to snap pictures with my phone, but the sight of family and friends gathered together was too awesome to view through a lens. A few people belted out a rousing rendition of "The Christmas Song" along with Nat King Cole, whose voice poured through the speakers. *Chestnuts roasting on an open fire.* Their voices rose in unison with the first word of every line, and I laughed along with them.

Could life be any better than this? Max and Margaret stood in front of the Christmas tree in animated conversation, and my own lips twitched as Max's eyes lit up with something his grandma said. Mom and Dad were listening intently as Sean, his arm around Fiona, talked to them. If anyone could convince them of the gospel, it was him. Tess regaled Maris with baby pictures while Katie and Tony led a group of Bella Cucina employees in a blind taste test of the foods laid out buffet-style on the dining room table. Jaime, the head waitress, had a scarf tied around her eyes.

"Are you hiding away up here?" Marty's voice startled me, and I looked up to find him looming over me from the top of the stairs.

Hand to my chest, I laughed. "Where did you come from?"

He jerked a thumb over his shoulder. "I was helping Jake put the baby down in Max's room."

"Max's room? Since when?"

"Ask him." He sat down next to me. "He's been telling

everyone that it's his room. Even brought Margaret up earlier to show her."

"It sure didn't take him long to stake a claim, did it?" I swung my head back around to observe the party again. "Thanks for letting me do this, Marty."

"Everyone seems to be having a good time." He pointed to the group with Katie and Tony. "What're they doing?"

"Their own rendition of *America's Test Kitchen*."

"So, why are you sitting here instead of enjoying the party?"

"Believe me, this is fun too." I held up my phone. "I was going to take pictures but got sidetracked with just watching." I shifted so my back was against his chest as he put his arms around me. "I don't remember ever having a Christmas party before. I think we should make this an annual event."

"I like the sound of that." His breath sent a shiver up my spine.

"Well, what do you say to——"

My phone vibrated in my hand.

I checked the screen and frowned. "Stephen."

"I'll give you some privacy." He planted a kiss on my temple before rising. "You should invite him over. Maybe Sean can work his magic on him, too."

I wanted to ignore it. It's not like he couldn't leave a message. But then Margaret's eyes met mine over Max's head, and she smiled. On the fourth ring, I answered. "Stephen?"

"Hey, Jules." I could just make out his words over the noise of the party crowd. "Did I interrupt something?"

Didn't he know his mother was here? "We're in the middle of a Christmas party. What's up?"

Silence.

Hoping to drown out some of the noise, I pressed my ear closed with a finger. "Are you there, Stephen?"

"Didn't mean to interrupt. Can you call me back in the morning?"

"Hold on." I jumped up, climbed the stairs and stepped into Celia's old room. The noise level dropped considerably. "Okay, that's better. What's going on?"

"I was hoping it would be okay if I see Max tomorrow."

Thank you, Lord.

"Look, I know you're mad at me," He rushed ahead. "And I get it, Jules. I do. But Max is all I have left." His voice cracked. "I've been doing a lot of thinking the last few days. There's not much else to do here at my mom's. I polished off her list of repairs my first day, and I haven't been able to find a job yet. I'm hoping after the holidays...anyway, I don't want to blow my relationship with Max."

I'd heard that one before, but it seemed like God was working miracles this season. "I'm sure Max would love to see you tomorrow. He has church in the morning, though." I held my breath. Stephen's habit was to mock my insistence on Max attending service.

"No, I know. I thought I could pick him up around noon and bring him back to my mom's for lunch. I'd take him out, but I'm sure she'd like to see him, too." He didn't have to remind me he was broke.

"Actually, Stephen, your mom is here."

"At your party?" He couldn't have sounded more surprised if I told him Santa had just slid down the chimney.

"Yes. She didn't tell you where she was going?"

"She probably thought it would be too awkward."

I felt as if God hovered over one shoulder and the devil over the other—One wanted me to offer grace and the other to fail at it. If at all possible, I was going to stick with Team God. "Max is here, too. You're welcome to join us. There's plenty of food."

He didn't say anything for a heartbeat or two. "I'm sure that would thrill Marty."

"It was his idea, Stephen."

"Why am I not surprised?" He sounded sincere. "Good

for you, Jules. Anyway, I think I'll just hang out here tonight. I'll pick Max up at your place at noon tomorrow?"

"Sounds good."

I headed back downstairs to join the party. It was six weeks ago to the day that Stephen and I were at Apple Hill Farms. Six weeks ago that Tess had given birth to baby Sean. Six weeks ago when I hadn't given Marty any more thought than as Jake's comic sidekick. I hadn't been talking much to Margaret, and I'd merely tolerated my parents. How was it possible that six weeks could change the entire trajectory of my life?

There is a time for everything, and a season for every activity under the heavens.

ABOUT THE AUTHOR

Jennifer Sienes holds a bachelor's in psychology and a master's in education but discovered life-experience is the best teacher. She loves Jesus, romance and writing—and puts it altogether in inspirational contemporary fiction. Her daughter's TBI and brother's suicide inspired two of her three novels. Although fiction writing is her real love, she's had several non-fiction pieces published in anthologies including two in *Chicken Soup for the Soul*. She has two grown children and one very spoiled Maltese. California born and raised, she recently took a step of faith with her real-life hero and relocated to Tennessee.

Visit her at https://www.jennifersienes.com/

facebook.com/Jennifer-Sienes-Writer-186643172596

instagram.com/Jennifer_Sienes

goodreads.com/Jennifer_Sienes

bookbub.com/authors/jennifer-sienes

pinterest.com/jennifer_sienes0101

ALSO BY JENNIFER SIENES

The Apple Hill Series

Surrendered (Book One)

Illusions (Book Two)

Providence (Book Three)—Coming Soon!

Celebrate Lit Publishing
Is proud to endorse

Finding the pictures to capture your words

http://www.roseannawhitedesigns.com/

ALL THAT GLITTERS COOKIE COOKBOOK

VARIOUS AUTHORS

JENNIFER SIENES' MOCHA WALNUT COOKIES

Ingredients:

12 ounce package of Dark Chocolate Morsels, divided
2 tbsp Instant Coffee
2 ¼ cups All-Purpose Flour (if gluten-sensitive, you can substitute Pamela's gluten-free all-purpose flour or any other 1:1 ratio gluten-free flour
¾ tsp Baking Soda
½ tsp Sea Salt
½ cup Butter, softened
½ cup Granulated Sugar
½ cup Brown Sugar, firmly packed
1 Egg
½ cup Chopped Walnuts

Directions:

Preheat oven to 350 F

. . .

Melt ½ C. chocolate morsels in double-boiler. Stir until smooth. Cool to room temperature. *see note below

In a small bowl, combine flour, baking soda, and salt. Set aside.

In a large bowl, combine butter, granulated sugar, brown sugar, and coffee. Beat until creamy.

Add egg and melted chocolate morsels. Mix well.

Gradually add flour mixture.

Stir in remaining 1 ½ C. chocolate morsels and walnuts.

Drop by rounded tablespoonfuls onto ungreased cookie sheets.

Bake at 350 for 10-12 minutes. Allow to stand two to three minutes before removing from cookie sheets. Cool completely.

Yields about two dozen 3-inch cookies.

*Although the preferred method for melting chocolate morsels is a double-boiler, I have done it directly in a non-stick pot on low. Just watch closely that the chocolate does not burn.

CAROLYN MILLER'S GINGER CHRISTMAS COOKIES

Ingredients:

5 ounces Butter
1 cup Brown Sugar
1/2 cup Golden Syrup (or Treacle)
1 tsp Ground Cinnamon
2 tsp Ground Ginger
1 teaspoon Ground Cloves
2 Eggs
2 tsp Vanilla Essence
4 cups Flour
2 tsp Baking Powder
Icing to decorate

Directions:

Melt the butter, brown sugar, treacle, cinnamon, ginger and cloves in a saucepan over a medium heat. Set aside.

. . .

Stir in the eggs and vanilla essence. Stir in the flour and baking powder until smooth. Divide the dough into 3 portions. Wrap in plastic wrap and refrigerate for at least 2 hours or until firm.

Preheat oven to 350°F. Line two baking trays with nonstick baking paper. Roll out 1 portion of the dough between 2 sheets of baking paper. Use Christmas cookie cutters to cut out biscuit shapes. Place on the trays.

Use the end of a piping nozzle to make a hole in the top of each biscuit. Bake for 5-10 minutes or until golden and firm. Repeat with the remaining dough portions. Transfer to a wire rack to cool.

Decorate with icing, silver balls and other edible decorations. Thread with ribbon to hang on the Christmas tree. Enjoy!

ALEX JACOBSON'S AUNTIE TONI'S SUGAR COOKIES

Cookie Ingredients:

1/2 cup Butter, softened
    1/2 cup Crisco
    1/2 cup Sugar
    1/2 cup Powdered Confectioners Sugar
    WHIP well

Then add
    1 Egg
    1 1/2 tsp Vanilla Extract
    1 1/2 tsp Almond Extract
    Beat wet ingredients till fluffy

In a separate bowl mix dry ingredients
    2 1/2 cups Flour
    1/2 tsp Baking Soda
    1/2 tsp Salt
    1/2 tsp Cream of Tartar

Add slowly to wet ingredients.

Directions:

You can then roll into balls and flatten with the bottom of a cup or glass OR refrigerate for 2 hours and then roll out and use a cookie cutter.

Cookie Icing Ingredients:

Confectioner's Sugar
  Water
  Milk
  Almond Extract

Directions:

This recipe is a bit trickier – especially if you are one who wants specific instructions. I put about 3 cups of confectioner's (powdered) sugar in a bowl add a teaspoon of water and a teaspoon of milk. Plus a half a teaspoon of almond extract. Then add milk and water alternating until it is a texture I want. You can always add more sugar to get it a bit thicker but remember – a little liquid goes a long way.

NYLA KAY'S CRANBERRY OATMEAL DELIGHTS

Ingredients:

1/2 cup Butter, softened
2/3 cup Sugar
1 Egg, slightly beaten
1/2 tsp Ground Cinnamon
1 tsp Dried Orange Rind
1 3/4 cup Flour
1 1/3 cup Old-Fashioned Oatmeal
1 tsp Baking Soda
1 tsp Almond Extract
1 tsp Orange Extract
1 cup Dried Cranberries
1/2 cup White Chocolate Chips

Directions:

Preheat oven to 350 degrees. In a large bowl, beat together butter, sugar and egg until smooth and creamy; stir in extracts & rind. In a separate bowl, mix together cinnamon, flour, oatmeal and baking soda until well-combined. Gradually add dry mixture to butter mixture. Stir in dried cranberries and white chocolate chips until blended. Drop dough by rounded teaspoons onto cookie sheet coated with nonstick cooking spray or parchment. Bake for 10 to 12 minutes.

Yields 3 dozen

LINDA MATCHETT'S CHRISTMAS SANDLING COOKIES

Ingredients:

½ cup Sugar

   2 sticks Butter

   2 Egg Whites

   2 cups Flour

   ½ tsp Lemon Rind

   ½ tsp Vanilla

   Decoration: chopped or whole pecans, candied cherries, or chocolate chips in center of flower "petal."

Directions:

Whip sugar and butter until white and fluffy. Add other ingredients except nuts and mix well. Fill pastry bag with batter, and using desired tip, force through bag onto ungreased cookie sheet.

. . .

Decorate as desired. Bake at 325 degrees for 12 minutes, rotating cookie sheet halfway through. If dough gets too warm, chill slightly in the refrigerator.

Yields approximately six dozen

MARGUERITE GRAY'S
CHRISTMAS SUGAR COOKIES

Ingredients:

1 cup Butter
   1 cup Sugar
   1 Egg
   2 tbsp Sweetened Condensed Milk
   1 tsp Baking powder
   ½ tsp Baking soda
   ½ tsp Salt
   1 tsp Vanilla or Almond Extract
   3 cups Flour

Directions:

Mix well, cover, and refrigerate at least an hour.

Roll out and use cookie cutters for Christmas shapes.

. . .

Bake at 400 degrees and watch—4-5 minutes,

Decorate with icing and sprinkles, candies, etc.

SANDRA BARELA'S
CHOCOLATE CHIP RECIPE

Ingredients:

2 1/4 cups Flour
   1 tsp Baking Soda
   1 tsp Salt
   1 cup Butter, softened
   3/4 cup Sugar
   3/4 cup Brown Sugar
   1 tsp Vanilla
   2 Eggs
   2 cups of Chocolate Chips

Directions:

Heat oven to 350 degrees.

Mix together flour, salt, baking soda in a bowl by hand and set aside until later.

. . .

In a stand mixer or in a bowl using hand blender, beat butter until soft, white and fluffy. scrape sides.

Add white sugar; beat until white and fluffy. Scrape sides.

Add brown sugar; beat until fluffy. Scrape sides.

Add eggs and vanilla. Mix on low in until just blended. If you over mix, your cookies will be tough. Scrape sides.

Add 1/3 of the flour, mix on low until blended. Scrape sides. Add another 1/3 of the mixture, mix on low until blended.
Scrape sides. Add last third of flour mixture and mix on low until blended. Scrape sides.

Add chocolate Chips and mix until blended (if using a hand mixer, mix chocolate chips in by hand).

Scoop onto cookie sheet and back for 10 min or until sides of cookies are firm.

Enjoy!

Made in the USA
Las Vegas, NV
01 November 2020